Limerence

Ashraf Elia

First paperback edition March 2019

Book cover. Danaë, by Gustav Klimt, 1907.
Galerie Würthle, Vienna, Austria

ISBN-10: 1797465481
ISBN-13: 978-1-7974-6548-7

For Her.

Lim.er.ence

/'limerens/

noun
the state of being infatuated or obsessed with another person. (usually involuntary)

PART ONE

She was on all fours on a bed, blindfolded, completely nude except for a wide leather collar around her neck. Behind her, a man she could not distinguish. But she knew he was handsome, powerful. She wanted him like she had never wanted anyone before. He played with her orifices. She was hot. She was sweating. Finally, he sank into her, gripping her hips firmly with his strong hands. She was savoring his cock, as it slowly penetrated deeply, her belly coming to contact with her swollen lips. She felt him fill her completely; she was physically fulfilled, overwhelmed by a huge wave of pleasure.

He quickly took a faster pace, ardently sliding in and out of her: a precise, mechanical gesture, but without any regard to her. She was also moving her ass to sink on him again and again, following his emotionless orders. She was panting and moaning, clenching her hands on the sheet; unconcerned with her screams of pleasure, she became lost in his movements, overwhelmed by this growing excitement. He took her from a more brutal approach, sometimes slipping his hand under her breasts to knead them and pinch her nipples. He was pulling her head back, sinking his fingers in her mouth. He caressed and slapped her cheek. He was playing with her sensations. And then he retook his position, slamming her ass violently, to encourage her to move faster on his cock.

She tried to stifle her cries, mixing Yes! Again! Again! with her groans. She did not know where she was, nor what she did. He put his hand firmly between her shoulders, pushing her flat to make her bend her elbows, her plump breasts forced against the bed. She was shamelessly arched, rump completely offered, as he continued to pound her, faster, deeper, more intensely than before. His hands clutched at her hips so hard that he hurt her, but she loved to feel his physical grip. He dominated her with all his might, only letting go of her to slap her ass, a slap much harder and much louder than she would have imagined, beyond the simple slap. He hurt her, she felt her ass blush, her skin warm. But she liked that. She loved it … She would have liked to live that way.

Apollonia opened her eyes and got up, wet. She was alone. The only pleasure she had taken was the one she had given herself with her fingers. Her fantasies and desires were becoming more and more intense, more and more uncontrollable, more and more frustrating. But she did not just want sex, let alone with anybody. She got up and turned off her computer, annoyed. She had not read what she hoped to have read, and she was disappointed. It had been like this for over ten days now, and she was starting to worry that it would always be this way. She measured her dependence, this visceral need to connect and to feed on his words, or a photo posted that may not even be him. She realized that this was what kept her spark alive, which gave her a taste for life.

Every day she imposed an identical ritual. She refrained from going to the Master Vincent's blog until the night, where she would savor it in her own quiet and calm environment, alone, always anticipating a new post from him. It was not even an email that had been personally sent to her, but only a few words posted publicly on a web page, accessible to anyone. She had been feeding on this for several months. It delighted her, and she enjoyed it as if it were a sweet drug. She quickly went through the whole text to know the length of it, then she lingered over the photos, if there were any posted. Then she started again, reading slowly, enjoying every word, soaking up the atmosphere he created. She imagined all the scenes and pictured what he described. Sometimes she broke off from reading to close her eyes, just to visualize and feel through his words: the intensity of the acts, the weight of the silence. The disappointment when there was nothing was the measure of her pleasure.

She often kept her thighs open, imagining that he forcefully caressed her as she read. She felt privileged to know so much about him. And then she snapped back to reality: everyone could know of him since it was a public blog. She had no favorable treatment, no particularity. She lurked in the shadows, secretly, admiring the stories written by someone she had never met, taking on the essence of his fantasies. She revered him as a god and did not consider him a man. He was above that, above the others. Beyond everything. Incomparable. Different. Was it because he was just answering all her veiled desires, these shameful cravings that she had been having for months?

She was not ashamed now, she knew that he would understand, that he knew what was in her, at the deepest part of her body and her soul. But to feel understood was not enough to adulate someone in that way; there was something else, she was certain. But what? She did not know. She did not care. She loved him without ever having seen him; too bad if someone thought this was ridiculous, no one knew anyway. It was her secret place and she felt wonderful when she was there. Alone in front of her computer, reading and rereading, almost touching the screen with her fingertips when she saw a glimpse of him in a picture. She read and decrypted the comments that ran through his stories, always women, who flattered and incensed him. Always a small band of groupies, with the most explicit allusions. Some played a lot on unspoken words and innuendo. They suggested that they had shared many things together, and knew each other intimately, outside of the blog. But Apollonia had learned which ones were true, and which were simple fantasies. More were only mere readers; far from this universe which nevertheless bewitched them, they gave themselves up to dream while letting themselves be enveloped with his words that sounded so right, sighing with desire. But it was obvious that they would never go beyond the stage of the diligent reading, and they did not hide it.

Apollonia did not really know where to go. She felt she did not fit into any of these categories. Besides, she never commented, she stayed in the shadows. She questioned whether she was a mere reader or a fantasist. And if she was, was she one of those who would be able to act as such, or would she remain permanently away from this world? She did not really know. She felt different. Linked in a particular way to this Master who was ignorant of her existence. Maybe she was afraid of the disappointment that would happen during a conversation with him, lest the myth collapses, losing its potency. Afraid that the Master's aura would fade. She preferred not to know him, rather than be disappointed. Yet she knew deep inside her that there was no real possibility of them interacting. He was so perfect in her eyes, always using the right words and demonstrating that charm and charisma in each of his publications, that she knew she would be a disappointment to him. Afraid that she would remain anonymous and insignificant in his eyes—just like so many others.

One of the others. She preferred to be nothing rather than one of the others. That's why she refused to leave a few words on his blog, and refused to contact him via a private message. She knew that he was within reach, so easy to contact ... but she did not want to be confronted with banal exchanges. She did not want to feel his disinterest and weariness grow as they continued to converse. She did not want to count the hours she would wait for an answer to an email. She did not want to torture herself and wonder if she did well, or whether her words had been well interpreted or not. She did not want to be the same as the others. She did not know how to get his attention, and she was afraid that she would fall back into oblivion after a few days or weeks. To be nothing anymore. To be even less than that, just another name that would be added to so many others in an already well-supplied contact list. Apollonia did not want to confront this reality. She preferred to remain invisible and convince herself that sooner or later their paths would meet if it were to be so.

A week or more between posts was becoming the norm, but his words still held the same power over her. She would have liked to read indefinitely, like an endless story. Sometimes she read everything from the beginning; each story was saved on her PC and even if the blog were to disappear, she would have something left of him. Month after month, she had kept every line, every photo, every comment. She knew everything about him; at least, everything he had chosen to disclose. She had not just read, she had learned and studied every detail; she knew what he loved, she knew his habits. She knew his preferences and requirements, the way a submissive was to talk to him, if she could or could not look at him, what position he preferred to take her, and what he liked her to do for him. She knew the kind of lingerie or clothing that he liked, the gestures or appropriate behavior in his presence, and the mistakes he considered inadmissible. She could have guessed in advance the punishment he would give for certain mistakes, even if they sometimes surprised her.

She felt close to him knowing so much, but deep inside her she knew he had not said everything. That there were a lot of details that she would never read through his stories. And then there was everything else. She did not even know what he really looked like; even if she guessed his looks through his descriptions, there was a chance that he may not be beautiful. Everything that came out of his texts showed an extraordinary self-assurance, unpretentious, but obvious. And even though she had repeatedly tried to imagine him as ugly to detach herself from him, she could not bring herself to believe that it was so. Words did not say everything. Apollonia did not know his scent, she did not know what colour his eyes were. She did not know if she would like the touch of his skin, the feel of his hair. She also did not know if she would be able to give him pleasure. She could not imagine how his moods were reflected on his face. She did not know how he smiled when he was joyous, nor the darkness of his eyes when he was angry. She did not know his voice, nor the exact intonation that he gave, according to what he wanted to express. She guessed it. The real him was not that artistic sketch in her thoughts; that was a shadow, a silhouette without a face, without a smell or voice, which dominated her in her fantasies. He was a superior spirit, an evanescent, immaterial being, divine without identity, just a dream.

The next day, nothing new appeared on her screen. The blog had not been updated. Frustrated at not being able to enjoy a new text, she again read one of her favorites. It was a few months old, and he was describing an exhibition scene he had with one of his submissives. She knew the words by heart, but still took pleasure reading them again. She already knew that after she would go lie naked on her bed and would imagine herself in his hands, at his mercy and under his control. She would imagine being the one he was talking about in the story, focusing on every little detail, admiring him. She offered herself to him and he received her as a sweet gift, respectfully and with full awareness of the value. Perhaps it was this respect she found so beautiful in these relationships. To be respected by a man who she would consider a god, lowering herself to him in worship. Feeling that you are important to someone you worship would make you feel like you could move mountains. Maybe that was what she needed, to be respected by someone like him. Maybe that would compensate for the lack of recognition and lack of consideration she had experienced throughout the years?

Without doubt that was a reason, but not the sole reason. It was a complex chemistry that attracted her and seemed to be the answer to all her questions. Apollonia understood— her head full of the words and images she so loved, this temptation was born in her. She closed her eyes and soaked up the imaginary world in which she was his. She mentally conceived the decor of this club where she had never been, but that she could imagine down to the smallest detail. She yearned for the feeling of being there, to have the eyes of the regulars on her. She imagined the moments of panic when he would dryly order her to remove her last pieces of lace, baring her naked body to all. She imagined herself flinching, feeling a chill as he inspected her body, examined it. In her thoughts, she was scared but she remained dignified, as he expected her to, and she obeyed: short breaths, slowly undressing, calmly following his orders to the letter.

With a head full of these dreams, with a body excited by these imaginary sensations, she slowly opened her legs and slid her hand between. She acted with restraint, as if she was really in the club, being judged on her submissive qualities, as well as her Master being judged on his training qualities. She wanted to please him more than anything, so she ignored her modesty and opened herself wider, arching her back. Her middle finger was rolling on her swollen clit, already wet with desire. She moaned gently and imagined his words, deliciously belittling, and yet revealing his full satisfaction with this obedience—without limits. She gently contorted with pleasure, imagining the eyes on her, oppressive, hard, watching for imperfections and seeking fault. But in her dream, she would not falter or close her legs, offering herself to her Master's desire, to this shameless exhibition. She would not comment or think, she would not be afraid of criticism or judgments, she would only obey. Obey him. After a public display as delicious as it was shameful, she would lift her eyes and see his pride at her overcoming this test. Nothing else would matter. She caressed herself until she orgasmed, not holding back, groaning and sighing until she opened her eyes. She was at home. Alone. Again.

Sometimes she was comfortable with that, and sometimes it was difficult. And that night it was difficult. She felt more humiliated than if she had been in the club, being forced to masturbate in front of everyone's eyes. The more time that passed, the more she felt as if she was not truly alive. She felt deeply lonely, non-existent. Her addiction to this blog, and her fascination for this Master took all her strength, all her energy. Little by little, she had closed herself to the rest of the world. She knew how others felt, full of prejudices, always quick to criticize what they do not know, or what was scary. Easy shortcuts, free critics, and heavy and coarse jokes, she had heard too much when she attempted to speak about it with others. Deviance, perversity, abnormality, and even madness were words applied to her desire to be submissive. It was not normal for a woman to submit, after all that had been done for the equality of the sexes! These slaves had problems, they had been abused children, obviously! She was shocked and appalled by all this, the lack of openness. The more she attempted to explain how she felt, the more she was looked at with suspicion, as if she became a carrier of a contagious disease. So, she had shut up and had chosen to pretend she was "normal." But she started to have less and less in common with those with whom she rubbed shoulders. She was alone in her fantasy world, with her desires unfulfilled. This faceless figure seemed to save her, soothing her until she felt well. She lived alone in the shadow of this Lord and Master, which would probably never be hers. But even so, it was enough.

†

Apollonia finally relaxed, slipping into a hot shower. She went out and observed her body in the foggy bathroom mirror. She was not indulgent with herself, but objectively she was rather well formed. Not exceptional, but without real defects. She had long legs, small, perky breasts, and her skin was milky, the sun never managing to give her the golden skin which she desired. She instead tended to become sunburnt easily and she often avoided exposing herself. Her buttocks, however, were rather well rounded, good enough that she imagined her Master would enjoy if she were to bend over in front of him.

Her face did not betray her age, and she was always judged younger than she was, even though she was barely thirty years old. She approached the mirror to observe her face, devoid of any makeup, and her brown eyes with amber reflections which always got some compliments; she knew her face was a major asset. She unraveled her blonde hair, which also contained a red shade, which she knew he enjoyed. She would have dyed it without hesitation, otherwise. She would have liked it to be smooth and straight, but instead, it was rebellious and impossible to style correctly, so most of the time she kept it simply tied up without attempting to tame it further. Despite all her positives, she did not feel like she could please him. She was not worthy.

She pleased men, certainly, but he was not like others, he

could not be satisfied with someone ordinary. She did not enjoy the feeling of judging herself as not beautiful enough for him; however, the opposite would have seemed extremely pretentious to her. She put on a T-shirt that fell to just above her knee, sat down in front of the TV, and wrapped herself up in a blanket. She did not want to think about him anymore, not tonight, but she knew that it was impossible. Apollonia went to bed late, after consulting the blog for one final time, but it had still not been updated since the previous week.

She thought of everything that had happened during this period. All that he had done and said that she would never know. She could see herself as his slave because he sometimes evoked his desire to own one. He sometimes wrote how he imagined it, and what his conditions would be. This slave would be constantly available, at any moment, to satisfy all needs of her Master. An indefinite slave, more present in his life than anyone else, sometimes adored, sometimes simply objectified. A slave without rights or freedom, who would curl up at his feet when he allowed it, and over whom he would rule without limits or restrictions. Apollonia shivered with excitement. Just imagining that place made her senses go wild, giving birth to an insane, unquenchable desire. She did not consider it at all too extreme.

And yet, deep inside her, she knew she hid the truth. She was in denial of her deep desires. She knew it, it rumbled in her, it was there, permanently. Intensely. She imagined more and more often. A slave. Even by just saying that to herself she wanted to be one; however, she knew that it came with many, many constraints, and wondered if she would be able to handle it. Yet she loved to imagine lying down at the foot of his bed, every night, available for anything that could go through his head. She was dreaming of being the slave of yesteryear, without the right to speak, eyes always lowered, always kneeling or prostrating at his feet.

The more time that passed, the more these fantasies intensified, and her stomach knotted in need. She herself could not explain it. How could she justify the desire to be deprived of freedom? How to justify the excitement to be enslaved more than a domestic animal, to live cloistered without a social life, without intimacy, constantly under orders, lowered, perhaps even struck? To be only a sexual object, a maid, a toy? She was searching herself, and she could not find the reasons behind her feelings. She had never been abused as a child, she had never been humiliated at school, she had not been raped as a teenager either, and had no conflictual relationship with her father, so why? Why did she have such desires? And why should there be a painful past to justify it? Was she finally like the others, convinced that only some psychotic problems could explain such inclinations? Certainly not, no. She was perfectly normal to want to be a submissive, fully dominated by a man. This was a sexual preference. But being a slave was more than that. It was less defensible, less justifiable. And yet, it did not leave her thoughts.

Apollonia had to wait four more days before finally seeing something new on Master Vincent's blog. He described the departure of his submissive after an intense session, and this was written after, when he was alone. He was talking about her fragrance that floated gently in the air, places of his home that still bore her imprint. He was seeing himself looking at her smiling at the metal ring attached to the ceiling where she spent many, many hours. She closed her eyes and imagined again the scenes which he described with precision. Then toward the end of his story, he again alluded to the fact that he would have liked a submissive or a house slave, who would sleep at the foot of his bed, whom he would make use of excessively, at any time of the day and the night.

Apollonia felt less shameful about this fantasy of belonging, discovering it was a fantasy shared and displayed by another. She sensed that she was no longer trying to justify the Master's interest, as it was plain to see. She wanted to live under these conditions, probably not for a lifetime, but for several months, maybe a few years. Sometimes she imagined herself being abducted by force, and forced into this life, without it being a choice. It was a way to exculpate herself and not feel responsible for this life of constraints. But that did not really make sense, she knew it. Time passed, and she still had the desire burning deep inside her. One of the comments under the story was written by Diane, the subject that was mentioned in the text. She mentioned her deep desire to be submitted to him permanently and regretted that she was not able to do so, because of family and other obligations. Apollonia realized that, in fact, few women could have gone beyond just wanting to become a slave. It was necessary that one did not have any emotional bonds. One should not wish to pursue a professional activity, or even any interests at all. Unemployed, she could not keep her home, or even maintain a minimum wage. The Master should therefore want to and be able to totally take control of her. And if overnight he did not want her anymore? Then she would end up with nothing—no work, no shelter.

She understood that owning a slave was not just a formality, even for a Master as he. If he did not have one, it probably was not by choice, but because he had not found the one that was to occupy this place. All this obsessed her for a long time. She was relishing in those thoughts and could not help but see a sign, a call. Impossible. It was impossible. Even if he wanted her.

Though thinking about it, she had had no regular contact with her family for a long time, and they would not worry. As for friends, she did not really have any, just acquaintances, people which she appreciated. Since the discovery of her penchant for submission and her desires to belong to this world, she had detached from the rest of the world, so that she would feel no frustration, nor be patronized by anybody. She had some money on the side, just a little, but enough to not be completely helpless after. And then she could certainly sublet her studio without any problems, as well as ask for leave without pay. She could claim to take a sabbatical year to travel the world.

Apollonia felt a little uncomfortable, troubled, disconcerted to recognize the feasibility of this project. She had of course realized that there would be many details that would complicate things, but there was always a means, a solution, a way to iron out the difficulties. She had to go and live this life, she had to become the slave of this Master who made her fantasize so much. However, she remained convinced that he would not want her as she was too average, not pretty enough. There was also the fact she had not done this before. Yes, she had imagined all the situations, all the humiliations, and all the sufferings that could possibly befall her, but all of this was only a dream, a fantasy. She had never had to obey an order. She had never felt the lash of a whip on her skin. She had never had to endlessly stay in a waiting position; she had never been naked, exposed, or used as a sex object. She had never been forced into a ritual. She had never been forced to do anything. And yet, although she could list everything that she had not done, she felt the desire to be his. Yes, she was a novice, but she felt capable of it all, she wanted to live it. Needed to live it.

All this took over her life. She thought about it permanently, it obsessed her. She did not know how to enter this world, and especially, how she would bear a refusal if she could not. How could she express to him her desire to belong to him, more than any other? How could she reach him? She did not want to think about failing, but at the same time she understood that it may be a possibility. She was going crazy with desires and frustration. It took all her energy and all her strength to stay sane. If he rejected her, she would suffer like never before, but without doubt, she could move on to something else knowing that she had at least tried. If she did not do it, she would stay frustrated and would continually live in regret, spending the rest of her days wondering whether he would have wanted her. She had to know, to try, and accept his decision, whatever it may be.

Apollonia knew from his writings that he sometimes spent his Saturday nights in a Parisian BDSM club. According to his blog, it took place every month, or two months, sometimes even more sporadically than that. She had often wanted to go there, to meet him without him knowing who she was. Just to finally see him, to discover his face and his body. To hear the sound of his voice and to see him in action, unduly submitting one of his subjects. But she was afraid of being disappointed, and most of all, to be made only too aware of her own nonexistence. However, now that she had almost made her decision to offer herself to him, she could not conceive of doing it classically, in sending him an email. It was so expected and obvious. How many would he have received? How many messages of desire? How many messages from horny women flooded his inbox? It was way too commonplace. If she wanted to get his attention, and above all, show him her motivations, she had to go well beyond the conventional. She needed to surprise.

She made her decision. Every Saturday night, she would go to this club, and from opening to closing, she would wait for her Master. She did not know how to recognize him, but she was convinced that she would feel it deep inside her when it was him. And then, she had seen many pictures he submitted, and by those means, it would be easy to recognize him without much difficulty. Days passed, and her passion did not diminish. Having decided that she would go through with it, her impatience became uncontrollable. She felt the urgent need to meet him. It had to be done imminently, as someone else could take her place at any second and her chance would be lost. That's why she did not want to waste her time. She discussed the idea of a sabbatical year with her employer, something that surprised him because he could not imagine her as an adventurer, backpacking around the world. However, the idea was still agreed upon. Likewise, one of her colleagues, whose son was searching for an apartment, agreed to him subletting Apollonia's apartment. He only had a small salary, but Apollonia trusted his mother, and knew that the rent would be paid. Especially since she would be delighted to get rid of him, at least for a while, as she was getting sick of him being stuck in her family home. Everything fell into place with disconcerting ease. It was almost too easy. She did not care about the repercussions with her colleagues and her boss. She realized that her year out could be postponed or cancelled for many reasons. But this could not happen, she needed to present herself to Master Vincent with peace of mind.

†

Saturday finally arrived, and Apollonia was able to prepare for her first night in the BDSM club. She was very impatient and spent the afternoon shopping to find something to wear. Something which would please him. She knew he preferred black, short, tight dresses that made all parts of the body accessible. He also liked high heels, like all men. So, she bought a totally indecent dress, satin and lace, as well as a pair of satin pumps with huge stiletto heels, with a thong around the ankle, which, hopefully, would allow her to have better balance. In the evening, she took her time getting ready, as if she were certain that he would be there, precisely that evening, to confirm the notion that their paths were meant to cross, and that their destinies were intertwined. She combed her long hair, tied it, making sure that a few locks fell back and forth, in a falsely disheveled effect. She had made her eyes black, and her mouth red. The makeup of a girl of the night. She slipped on her dress and shoes, and observed herself for a long time in the mirror. I look like a whore, she thought, smiling to herself.

She hid her slutty attire under a long coat and got a taxi to avoid having to walk in her shoes which were going to be torture. The taxi stopped just in front of the club door. A door so innocuous that Apollonia was disappointed. Disappointed, but not discouraged. She swallowed her saliva and rang the bell, watching right and left, nervous—almost ready to see him emerge at this precise moment. However, he did not. Instead, a man opened the door, obviously surprised to see her alone, and seemed to hesitate a second, before courteously allowing her to enter. The man engaged in polite conversation, taking her coat, but she was too nervous to respond and was rather reserved. He did not insist but warned her that she was the first arrival. The club was just opening its doors.

She slowly descended the stairs that led into the main room of the club, and found a place of choice, with a perfect view of the stairs, but far enough away to not automatically attract the attention of anyone coming down. She felt uncomfortable being there. She should have discovered this place with him, if he so decided. She had the sensation of desecrating a sacred law, of not respecting the rules. She was going to discover the games, the roles, the codes of this world. She would meet the practitioners without even being introduced by her own Master; it was like cheating. She was organizing this meeting without it being his will. And if he disliked that? If he felt it strange that a reader of his blog were to confront him as such, without his knowing?

Apollonia's confidence began to fade. She felt like she was at fault, without being able to explain why. She was trying to justify, to remember her arguments. She did not want an ordinary meeting, over email, on a pixelated screen. But it was not what she wanted that counted, but what he wanted. How could she know what he would have preferred? She finally hoped that he would not come, then she would not come back either, and would stop this crazy quest. Yet she could not stop being disappointed every time she saw someone descend the staircase only to realize it was not him.

The evening went by, with the rhythm of arrivals and departures. Apollonia did not want to see anything else, she did not to intrude further into this world without being accompanied by him. She just wanted to meet him, breathe him, feel him, let herself be invaded by his aura. And if indeed she had confirmation of what she had been thinking from the beginning, namely that she had no other reason to exist than to belong to him, she would offer herself, even at the risk of being rejected in a public place. Several people had accosted her, some to converse or to offer a drink, others just curious about her attitude, thinking of an expectation imposed by a possible dominant.

She showed herself every time to be distant and withdrawn, so that they would become disinterested—but, of course, there were some men who seemed to believe that everything was owed to them, and that any single woman in this club was begging for his attention. She knew, however, to discourage them. The hours had passed, and nothing had happened. She had to face the facts: it was too late, and he was not coming. When she left, the man in the locker room tried to discover her reasons for attending.

"I was waiting for someone who did not come, I will come back next week," she revealed to him. Apollonia went back by taxi, as she had come, alone and a little distraught.

Then came two other Saturdays much in the same way. During all this time, the blog had not been updated, and Apollonia felt her faith falter. She cursed herself for not having acted sooner. Nothing, however, prevented her from sending an email, a simple message to tell him how much she would like to meet him, even for a moment, but she refused, without really being able to explain it. No doubt a virtual refusal would have been harder to take. No doubt she wanted to be afforded the opportunity to see the Master at least once. Only that. To share the same air, the same space. Being so close to him as to touch him and feel him. Burn his image deep inside of herself so that he would never again be a shadow. She probably wanted also to prove to herself, prove to him, that all this was not just fantasy. It was one thing to send an email from her sofa, it was another thing to come and kneel at his feet. She hoped it would touch him and show her seriousness in becoming his slave.

The fourth Saturday, finally, he arrived. She gasped and felt like she was going to faint. Her hands trembled, and she became full of nerves. She felt that she would never have the strength to do what she had planned. She did not see him at first. It was Diane she recognized. She had seen her in many pictures, in positions, most of the time. She found her even more beautiful in real life. She was graceful and slender. She was the very definition of femininity and classy, sexy elegance. She was perfect.

Apollonia felt there was a type of banal platitude to her. She did not take her eyes off her. She wore polished boots, platformed, which made her legs endless, and the fishnet stockings she wore did not seem vulgar, although her skirt was so short that she could see her suspenders. Her chest was highlighted by a very tight corset adjusted in such a way that it looked hard to believe she could breathe. Diane looked up as she came down the stairs, revealing a haughty expression and assumed pride. She was in her world, in a known land, on conquered soil. Apollonia could not remove her gaze from the wide leather collar she wore around her neck. The powerful leather she dreamed of day and night. She was moved and totally disconcerted, on the brink of tears as emotions jostled with each other inside her. But she suddenly came back to reality when Diane stepped forward, and the man behind her appeared to her finally. She felt her belly writhing and every inch of her began to tremble, and her soul burned. It was him.

No doubts possible. It was not only him, this Master about whom she had been reading stories for almost two years, but he was much more than that, he was more than what she expected, she felt. Her heart was beating so fast she felt it was going to burst.

She was perspiring. Her sweat quickly became cold, and she was frozen, unable to go and talk to him. She remained motionless for a long time, so that anyone who had observed her that night, and the previous Saturdays, would have instantly known that the one she wanted was in the room with her, only meters away. Apollonia exhaled softly, slowly regaining control of her body. This was it. She had imagined this moment hundreds, maybe thousands of times, and yet she felt helpless, as if she had forgotten everything. She did not know where she was, or why she was here. She could not pull herself together.

"Are you okay?"

Apollonia came out of her trance, a little haggard, looking for the source of these words which she knew had been addressed to her. She turned her head and saw a woman in her forties, her face round with red cheeks, all dressed in leather, looking visibly worried.

"Yes, I'm fine."

"Are you sure? You are very pale, I thought you were about to faint."

"Yes, I don't know what came over me, but I feel better now. Thank you ..."

Apollonia picked herself up, looking for him, but she could no longer see him. She panicked internally for a few seconds, when she finally saw him come back from the bar, two flutes of champagne in his hands. He sat down, and Diane knelt at his feet, with a naturalness that portrayed a great habit. Apollonia observed, admiringly. She was not jealous, but she would have given anything to be in her place. She stayed in this state for a while, thinking of what to do or what to say to this man, her potential Master. Then suddenly, without really thinking, she got up with a bound, and walked toward him. It was as if her body had taken the initiative to act, understanding that her mind would never strength to do so. She was right in front of him, almost surprised to be there, and he finally raised his eyes to look at her. She was no longer invisible. She was facing him. As if she suddenly realized where she was, she rushed to kneel awkwardly, her legs trembling because of nerves, or the six-inch heels she was wearing. She panicked, and wished that she could have just disappeared, that the ground could have swallowed her up and for him to forget about her. But she was there. She had to say something. Time seemed to be hanging, as if the music had stopped, as if people had stopped to listen to this long-awaited statement.

"Master, forgive me for disturbing you ... can I speak?" Her voice was whispering, trembling.

"I'm listening to you." She kept her head down, because if she had to lock eyes with him she would have lost all composure; she was already quite feverish.

"You do not know me, but I know who you are ... I ... I come to offer myself to you ..."

Silence. Her heart was beating like never before, she was shaking, she felt as if she were going to faint again. She was trying to control her breathing and get hold of herself. She guessed he was waiting for something else, other words, but nothing came out of her mouth.

"A very unexpected gift ... Look at me."

His voice ... his words, all for her ... She raised her head gently, then looked into his eyes. The first real look. She did not know what he read in her, but she was trying to convey what she was feeling in the depths of her soul, why she was there. He smiled slightly and told her that he was willing to have an evening with her. His words excited her terribly because they were addressed to her, but she realized that he had not understood. She felt uncomfortable. She had to react quickly.

"Excuse me, I did not express myself well ... it's not for the evening ... I offer myself completely ... I want to belong to you ..."

New silence. Weighing. Apollonia again lowered her eyes and even stopped breathing so everything seemed to be frozen. A chill went through her whole body. There must have been some noise around them, music, conversations, even shouting, most certainly, from nearby rooms. But she heard nothing but silence.

"It's tempting. But I already have a submissive," he said, exchanging a smile with Diane. Apollonia swallowed; this time it was she who caused the silence. She felt that her dream was vanishing, that everything collapsed. Everything that had kept her alive until now went up in smoke.

"I know, Master. I do not want to be your submissive, but your slave."

She bowed a little more in front of him, lowering her head as much as possible, her hands on the ground between his knees. This time the silence was worse. A tear crashed onto her hand before she managed quickly to pull herself together. If he told her no, she wanted to leave with her head held high, and certainly not the opposite, in a teary mess, eyes soaked, dripping with mascara.

"Are you really aware of what you propose to me?"

"Fully, Master." This time, her response had contained a surge of certainty and determination.

"Get up. And undress. Let's see what you have to offer me." Apollonia's throat tightened. She did not plan for this. She did not really plan anything, for that matter. She was too concerned with the request that she did not imagine what would happen after. She just thought that if he was interested, they would discuss it, he would ask her questions, and he would impose his conditions. And now, it was impossible for her not to obey his very first order. She got up, wobbling on her heels. She was facing him, as if there were no one else around them. She was not wondering what his submissive was thinking, still kneeling next to him, so close to him. Apollonia unbuttoned her dress and pulled it off with as much elegance as she could. She stood there, awaiting judgment.

"All of it. Off."

He already seemed to be losing patience. Did he just want to play with her? To ridicule her before rejecting her? She had no choice. She took her time and took off her underwear, her shoes, and her stockings. She felt eyes on her, they were heavy and oppressive. When she had walked toward him, no one was stripped, she must be the only one. If he accepted her request, he could order her to strip in the middle of the Champ-de-Mars, and she had to obey, so she had to show her strength. What was difficult for her was to be there, judged, without knowing. She was not exactly his. Not yet. She was completely naked in front of him.

The seconds went by. There must have been around twenty people around the two. Apollonia knew that this place was usually the theater of much more daring scenes and wondered what more he would ask for. She wanted to submit to him, but not to cause a scene. He watched her silently, and with attention. She felt like an object in front of him, and she had to admit that it was terribly exciting.

"Turn around."

She obeyed and remained with him what seemed like an eternity. She felt his hand brush against her back and hips, and that made her instantly shudder. She was still, but trembling, impatient for his verdict. And dreading it at the same time.

"In front of me." Apollonia turned around again, her throat still tight, short of breath.

"I'll think about it. Come back here, in a week, same time. I'll tell you then."

"Yes, Master."

"In the meantime, get dressed and leave."

"… Yes, Master." With these words, he got up without looking at her, and took his submissive upstairs, leaving Apollonia alone and naked in the middle of the room. It took a few moments for her to snap back to reality. She felt a little miserable getting dressed like that in front of so many sets of eyes. He did not tell her no, but she was not sure she could believe that the next week he would say yes. She left with her head down, without much hope.

This whole situation seemed unreal to her, so much so that she did not even know if she had really lived it or if it had been a fantasy, a dream. She had come out abruptly into the street, hastily even. She was out of oxygen, she was out of breath. The fresh air from outside did her good, but she was still sweaty, panting, as if she had run until she could not run any further. She was confused, disoriented. She was almost staggering, as if she had drunk too much. She called a taxi, thanks to the number stored in her phone, and leaned against the wall, still stunned by what she had done.

She tried to regain her senses. She had seen him. Finally. He was no longer a shadow, she did not dream all that. She knew it now. This Master existed. Beautiful and good. He was as she had dreamed; endowed with an uncommon charisma, he exuded a natural authority, an assurance mastered to perfection. All his gestures, his gaze, his posture, his voice was dripping with indescribable magnetism.

The silence he had created, the calm tone in which he had spoken without manifesting surprise or hesitation, everything had been exactly as she might have dreamed, and more. Sure, she had imagined that he would have spoken to her more, that he would have offered to discuss terms with her, to find out who she was, and why she wanted this. If it was realizable or not. She did not expect him to make her strip naked and send her away until next week. She had wanted to surprise him and accost him in his world, and she had to accept the rules in return. Maybe he was caught off guard and had chosen not to show it in opting for this solution. This allowed him not only to take the time to think, but also to test her motivations a little. No doubt he was not even sure that she would be at the rendezvous seven days later.

She felt as though it had only lasted a handful of seconds, that everything went very quickly despite the silences. She did not take enough advantage of the moment, of the delicious feeling she had felt when she knelt facing him, or when she felt the touch of his hand. His fingers slipping along her hip. Along her body. Her body next to his. He touched her, brushed her, caressed her with the tips of his fingers. He had seen her completely naked, without even asking her name. Just like that, because he had ordered it, she had undressed in front of all these strangers, almost naturally.

He had wanted her naked, so she had laid herself bare. As if this obedience was always anchored in her, waiting to finally be unleashed. She constantly replayed everything over in her head, the sensations, the emotions, contradictions, and excitement she had felt. It was as if she had taken a hard drug for the first time; she felt it unfurl into every aspect of her being, into each cell of her body, rooting itself. This was her addiction.

The taxi arrived, and she had trouble reacting to usual gestures and conversation as she was still feeling quite outside of herself. Could not even remember returning to her house. She loved the lights of Paris, but tonight it was he who grabbed her full attention. She saw only him, his image was planted in her mind, permanently: the expression on his face, the perfect mastery of the unforeseen situation. She saw his nose, his wide chin, the little wrinkles he had on either side of his dark-blue eyes. She was reviewing his brown hair, a little long, deliberately disheveled, and his two-day beard. He seemed to have come straight out of an ad for Hugo Boss, maybe a few years older. He was dressed in black, but she could not remember precisely what he wore, as for the majority of their exchange she kept looking down. She had not had the time to breathe his scent. She had not had time for so many things. She had found herself naked so fast, she had not controlled anything, only an incredible adrenaline rush had guided her actions.

Everything else was unclear. How she was dressed, how she opened the door of her apartment—she did not remember it anymore. It did not matter. She stayed like that, hanging on to her thoughts, for a good deal of the night, until the sun began to rise. She was looking for any reason why she should not follow this path, but she could not, as with such evidence, this man was for certain her reason for being. She smiled thinking about it, running her hand over her hips, where she still had the sensation of feeling the warmth of his hand. She rolled herself into a ball under her duvet, truly content.

†

Apollonia slept most of the day, so she was completely disoriented upon awakening. She wondered if she had dreamt it all or not. And then she realized, no, she had not. The shadow of her fantasies had a face, a look, and a voice. He was of flesh and blood. She knew he existed. He had caressed her skin, and in six days she would know. She rushed to her blog as soon as she could, but nothing had been added. It was too early. No doubt he had already forgotten this woman who made this crazy proposal out of nowhere. A man like him could easily forget such an experience. Can a Master be insensitive to a submissive kneeling at his feet, to give him her freedom? She did not believe so, no, but tried to convince herself to prevent her disappointment, in case he did not honor the appointment he had made. The week passed with a slowness which was out of the ordinary. Apollonia could not focus on anything, she begged for the days to pass, her whole being focused on the Saturday night which was slow to come. She bought herself another dress, so as not to appear to him in the same outfit. Every night she watched the blog, which seemed to be frozen in time. She started wondering if this was good or bad.

Saturday finally arrived. She was exhausted, she could not eat anything. She arrived at the opening hour, like the other times, under the gaze of the little surprised man who opened the door to her, as if he had not expected to see her again after her hasty departure the previous week. She remained silent, like the other times, but she was nervous and feverish. The man understood that this evening would be decisive, and it would be the last time that he saw her. At least in that way. Apollonia sat down in her usual place, but hardly dared to look up, wondering about her attitude if he did not come. Her heart pounded with the mere thought of sharing the same air as him again.

He did not arrive until late in the evening, as if he had wanted to torture her a little or play with her nerves. He was again accompanied by Diane, who attracted the looks of everyone in the room. He stopped in front of her, and remained thus, motionless. Quiet. Apollonia had lowered her head; sitting as she was, in front of him, she knew that if she had raised her head, if only a little, she would have had her mouth just a few inches from his penis. She shuddered in excitement and at the same time she was troubled and a little ashamed to have these thoughts in such an important moment.

"I did not think you'd be here."

"You had my word, Master."

"I see." A few seconds passed, that Apollonia dared not interrupt. She could not find the words, being too afraid they were not right. That they were not the ones he wanted to hear.

"Come."

He walked away, and she straightened up abruptly, breathless, fully aware that the minutes and maybe hours that were coming would be decisive, and that maybe her life was going to change completely.

Master Vincent went upstairs and entered a small room adorned with a cross of St. Andrew, and two large armchairs of red velvet, allowing people to attend the show offered on the cross. There was nobody there at that time, and he settled on the armchair, with a serene and assured air around him. Diane knelt to his left, always naturally and with elegance. Curious people peered in, but seeing that nothing was yet happening, they just stayed in proximity, ready to invite themselves into the room to become spectators, if it suddenly became more exciting.

Apollonia felt her heart throbbing in her chest, so strongly that she thought her pulse could be heard throughout the room. She knelt in front of him, head bent, buttocks on her heels, knees apart just enough so that she could put the palms of her hands on the ground. She had acquired this position naturally, finding it even more respectful than if she were to sit plainly on her knees. She wanted to discover these positions, and others, but she would have to wait for him to impose them if that was his will. As long as he did not order her to do anything specific, she was content to do what she hoped would please him.

He watched her for a long while, so long that she ended up asking herself if it was up to her to break the silence. In front of a king or a divinity, it is advisable to speak only if one receives the order; Apollonia also decided to remain silent so as not to risk committing an error. It could have also been a test on his part. So, it was finally he who broke the silence.

"Your request intrigues me. Have you ever been subjected to a Master?"

"Never, no."

"And you think you can be a slave?"

"Yes, Master."

"Are you aware of what this represents?"

"Yes, Master."

"I doubt it, to tell you the truth."

"I will show you, if you give me the chance, Master."

"If I accept your request, you will be a slave at home. No phone, no possibility to reach anyone. Without being able to go out whenever you like. You will have no freedom." Apollonia felt a long thrill of excitement run down her spine, leaving her with a warm feeling which spread through her whole body.

"Yes, Master. I am well aware of it."

"You have no family? No friends? No work?"

"I have no one really close, and I can find an arrangement for my work."

"Your accommodation? What would you do?"

"I can sublet, Master."

"I see you've already thought of everything."

"Yes, Master, I would not have allowed myself to offer myself to you without being completely prepared."

"I see. I usually choose who will be submitted to me, and I do not usually take the firstcomer. But your approach is different. I'm curious about you. But I will not commit myself for the moment. You will have to prove yourself."

"Yes, Master, thank you for allowing me."

"I'll take you on a trial. One week. If you give up during this week, you will leave as you came, and I will not ever see you again. You will have made me waste my time. If you want to stay all week, I'll tell you if I want to continue or not. And if this is the case, you can choose to stay. If it's not the case, you will be free to leave, with dignity. If you decide to continue, then we will extend it by one month, at the end of which I will repeat the question, under the same conditions. If I wish that you stay, and you too wish to stay, we'll extend for a year. And then stop there. I think it's appropriate for this situation. All this is not negotiable. You can still give up now."

"I will not give up, Master." Apollonia felt drunk and enveloped in a gentle warmth. He accepted her, at least on trial. An uninterrupted flow of images paraded before her eyes. All she had imagined and dreamed of living, mingled with the stories she had read, and with the images that had been born in her. She could not believe she was going to live as his slave. Finally.

"We will see. I have a very clear idea of what I want in a slave. As you are a novice, I will have to teach you everything. Do not waste my time. I will be very demanding, and I do not expect any complacency."

"Yes, Master, I will do my best to never disappoint."

"It will happen. Inevitably. Then you will suffer the consequences."

"Yes, Master, I understand."

"You do seem very receptive. You will come to this address next Saturday at nine o'clock in the morning. Just take what is necessary for a week. Be on time."

"Yes, Master."

"Leave us now. I do not want to start your education here."

"Yes, Master."

A second time, Apollonia had to leave, knowing that he would spend all night in this place. He was there, and she was leaving without turning back. As she waited for the taxi to arrive, she unfolded the paper he had given her and gave the address to the driver when he arrived. She wanted to know, to see. She still wanted to immerse herself in him and keep the image of what she was going to see at this address during the week that was going to pass. She wanted to make it all as much of a reality as possible, as she still struggled to believe it.

The taxi stopped in front of a beautiful Haussman building close to Odeon Place. She remained motionless, staring at length at the building before asking the driver to take her back to her apartment. She arrived home, her mind foggy, the way drunkenness leaves blank memories and that feeling of floating. But she no longer doubted the reality of all this. She had seen his building, she had read his words, which brought her to a place she would know in a week. She would be his in seven days' time.

The anxiety of not being able to satisfy him came to mind; deep inside her she felt like some assurance, although she would have refused to admit it. She felt so convinced she had been made to belong to him. And then she felt as if she was pretentious to have such thoughts; she persuaded herself that no, he would not like her, he would throw her outside within days, maybe even hours.

Apollonia had a week like never before, passing through all stages imaginable: renunciation, acceptance, conviction, doubt, excitement, impatience, and other states she could not even describe. On Saturday she was ready at seven in the morning; she had not slept because of the excitement she felt. It was not from sexual arousal, though, but mostly from waiting for what seemed so long. To please him, or not to please him. Was she going back head down, eyes puffy with tears in a few hours? Or would she leave for a new journey, in obscure countries, full of wonders, but also of difficulties, of a year or more? This uncertainty made her crazy; she had lost her appetite. She felt herself trembling, and her stomach began to knot.

At eight o'clock in the morning, she left her home, unable to wait there any longer; she preferred to wait in his neighborhood. She was immersed in this environment, an environment alien to her, but known to him. She wanted to laugh, to cry, to flee, to be there already. All at once.

At a quarter to nine she was standing under the porch, her finger ready to dial the code indicated on the paper. She asked herself again how she had resisted going to this place before today, showing up a few days early. But she had stood firm, fearing to ruin everything by arriving at a time which he did not agree on. She opened the heavy door and entered a beautifully paved courtyard.

A small haven of peace in the capital. She turned, found the main entrance, and climbed up the stairs to the top floor, carrying her little suitcase at arm's length. It was the standard cabin-size suitcase, which meant she did not take many personal effects. The grand stone staircase seemed to go on forever.

She was in a half-consciousness, everything was a blur. Then she arrived. Right outside his door. The door on the right, top floor. She looked at her phone. It was exactly nine o'clock.

She rang the doorbell.

PART TWO

When Master Vincent opened the door, Apollonia bowed her head, so much so that she would not even have noticed if it were not him. She remained motionless in the threshold, suitcase in hand, and seemed extremely fragile.

"Enter." Unable to articulate anything, she entered his home on her tiptoes, as one would enter a sanctuary or a holy place. She gasped, almost surprised that this was so easy ... almost disappointed that it was so easy ...

"Drop your suitcase."

"Yes, Master." Apollonia still had not looked up, for fear of committing any fault, which would have stripped away this opportunity completely. She could barely breathe. She put her suitcase by her side, barely bending her knees, and immediately resumed her position, humble and fixed. She felt his gaze on her. He watched as he would have done a wild animal, which he would have liked to study without his own actions influencing it. The silence was heavy. Despite her immobility, Apollonia was out of breath, praying internally for something to happen. Anything. Master Vincent ended up saving her from this eternal wait.

"I want you to listen very carefully to everything I tell you. I do not like to repeat myself."

"Yes, Master."

"You will have noticed that I did not ask you your name. I do not want to know. Do you know that in the past, one of the first things that was removed from a slave was their identity? Their name. This is meant to mark a before and after, a transition, break. If you stay, I'll maybe give you a name that will suit you, but I need to get to know you before this. In the meantime, I will call you Slave."

"Yes, Master." Apollonia shivered with excitement. She loved the sound of his voice, that voice that had for so long been a fantasy, an imagined voice. Now it was real, she could hear it. He spoke with the assurance of a man who is used to being respected and obeyed. He spoke to her. He was alone with her. He would call her Slave ... she was his slave. She repeated this to herself as if to be convinced of it as it seemed surreal.

"Your life will be reduced to many constraints, ungrateful tasks, and rituals. At any moment I can call on you—and you must obey. You will learn to do everything exactly as I want you to do it; otherwise, you will be punished. I hold every right over you, including the right to hit you, whether to train you or just for my pleasure. Do you understand all of this?"

"Yes, Master."

"You will have no freedom, no free time, no privacy. You will not have a place of your own. You will not choose the clothes you wear nor the food you eat. I will make sure that everything you do will be accompanied by a constraint, so that you never forget your condition. You will be a servant. Furniture. A decorative object. You will be a distraction for my friends. A sexual object if I have that desire. You will be invisible most of the time, acquitting yourself carefully in your obligations. But with the slightest mistake, you will be severely punished. On the other hand, if you give me satisfaction, I will also reward you."

Apollonia lowered her head a little more at these last words, as if the very idea of a reward seemed incongruous to her. She felt honored to be in this position, she felt unworthy. Yet she felt a kind of lightning of excitement in her belly, a small electric discharge of pleasure and need. She knew that if he had slipped his hand between her thighs, he would have felt that she was already wet, excited by the words that he spoke.

"You will serve me, from morning till night, and you will be at my beck and call, day and night, whether I want to fuck your mouth, or a cup of tea. You will sleep at the foot of my bed, on a dog bed, and if I do not want your company, you'll sleep in the hallway."

"Yes, Master."

"You will not have the right to speak without my permission. If you have something to say to me, you will come and prostrate yourself at my feet, and wait until I allow you to open your mouth. Then you can speak."

"Yes, Master."

"You will learn to walk in high heels, and you will wear them permanently while you are here. You will also learn to walk on all fours, like a dog. You will learn to dance lasciviously. You will learn the gestures which pleasure me. You will respect my submissive, who will not be your equal. She will have as many rights over you as I, if I see fit. If I order you to obey her as you obey me, you will. If you are not ready for this, leave immediately."

"I'm ready for anything, Master." Although this response had sprung from her mouth without even the time for reflection, Apollonia felt her throat tighten. She was not sure that she could obey Diane, or at least she was not sure if she wanted to. But she was ready to do it, and she must do it, if he so wished. She realized that she had not thought about it all. She had not planned for that, and suddenly, she was anxious at the idea of everything she might not have thought of. She nevertheless insisted on remaining impassive.

"On your side, you will have no rights over anyone. No one will ever feel belittled in front of you, but rather the opposite. I want unfailing obedience. I want to be able to demand everything from you. Anything. Otherwise, you will not deserve to be my slave. I want total abnegation."

"Yes, Master." He strode forward, and she followed him, mechanically. He showed her around his apartment, much like an estate agent, naming each room, allowing her to look around and inspect everything. The inventory was quickly established. The main room served as a living room and dining room There was a separate kitchen, a corridor, two bathrooms. There were also two bedrooms, one of which, his, had a bathroom and a large dressing room. Then they reached a small terrace, or balcony. Apollonia had been expecting something bigger, but she was still impressed. She would have been anyway.

She loved the decoration: simple, refined, and contemporary. Oak parquet original and the ceiling moldings strangely suited the modern furniture, with its straight edges and smooth material. Everything was of quality and good taste. When he got to his room, he showed her a bed for a dog. A large model, which looked comfortable, crafted from a smooth, black material. Apollonia could not hold back a smile, not only because she liked the idea of sleeping at the feet of her Lord and Master, but also because she thought he had bought it for her. He had thought of her during the week and went to a pet shop to buy this cushion, thinking forward to all those nights that she would spend at the bottom of his bed, so close to him. Available at any second.

He explained to her that she would not be allowed to use his bath, only the other one in the hall, and that she would have to leave the door wide open, as well as when she went to relieve herself. He added that all this would be subject to his consent, when he would be present, and that each time she needed to go she would need his permission. Apollonia shuddered. Of course, she was not surprised. The principle of intimacy did not exist when one was a slave, but to hear it said so concretely, so naturally, troubled her more than she would have previously believed. She was beginning to realize that going from fantasy to reality was far from being a formality.

Master Vincent opened her suitcase and looked at its contents. Mainly lingerie, some sexy outfits, and a makeup bag. He quickly sorted through everything, leaving some in the bag and bringing others with him to the bathroom, as Apollonia followed him, docile, like a lap dog. He created a little space for her belongings.

"You will not need a lot of room. You will almost always be naked. If you stay, I'll buy you more shoes and some outfits. Take off your clothes."

"Yes, Master." Apollonia's mind was racing, her stomach knotted, even though it was not the first time she was naked in front of him. He watched her, aloof and nonchalant, as she peeled her clothes off. He made sure that she knew that nobody would be able to reach her during this week, and he placed all her belongings, including her purse and suitcase, into a little cupboard in the hallway.

"I forbid you to go and take something without asking my permission, is that understood?"

"Yes, Master." Apollonia was standing, only wearing the suspenders, stockings, and shoes that she had purposely bought for him. Somehow, she felt even more naked than she had felt in the club. She instinctively bowed her head and her shoulders retracted, unintentionally rounding her back, as if she was trying to hide herself. Master Vincent seized the whip which had been sitting on the coffee table since her arrival and slowly approached her. He circled her, like a shark circling its prey, leaving her anxious of what he was going to do next. Then, without warning, a violent blow of a whip warmed her thigh, forcing a scream from her, a scream of surprise and pain. She gasped; her eyes widened as being struck only confirmed the feeling of foreboding she had had a little earlier. The reality of being a slave was going to be a lot different than she had previously imagined. The pain seemed to spread, radiating from where the leather had hit, and then almost immediately she felt nothing but a warm tingle.

"Straighten up!"

"Yes, Master."

Apollonia pulled back her shoulders so quickly that you would have thought she was standing to attention. She felt it was starting, that it was on the way. It was no longer a dream or a fantasy. It was no longer just a few words displayed on a computer screen. It was reality. Her reality. Her heart beat so fast she could hear it in her ears. She felt strangely good. In his element, at his mercy. Where she should be.

"You stand facing me, with straight shoulders and an arched back." His voice betrayed no anger but left no room for dispute. He was a teacher, holding a lesson that he may have had dozens of times, but he did not seem tired of it.

"I want your back arched. You will learn, and soon it will be a reflex, a natural posture. But in the meantime, you will be whipped every time I see that you are not in such a posture. Do you understand?"

"Yes, Master."

She threw her shoulders back; her breasts pushed forward, feeling more exposed than ever before. He wore black suit trousers and a white shirt, and this contrast between him and her, the smart clothes he wore and her nakedness, excited her. He gently stroked her breasts, making her shiver and repress a groan. Then his hand became firmer as he kneaded them, so hard it was almost painful, before pinching her nipples. Apollonia was challenged to remain impassive and show no pain or pleasure.

She had so often dreamed of living these moments. She knew that her body betrayed her, as much by her breath escaping from her ajar mouth as by her dripping wet pussy. Still, she wanted him to touch her, she wanted to feel his wide, powerful hands all over her body. She wanted him to be abrupt, dominant, insulting. She wanted him to take her, to have her, to fuck her. She wanted to feel like a bitch and a whore, to be just a body which he would use for his pleasure. Imposing himself on her, without delicacy, slamming her ass as much as he would like, which would make her scream as she had never screamed before in the presence of a man. She wanted him to use her and abuse her until he no longer wanted her.

Suddenly, all her frustration accumulated; all these months of abstinence came to the surface. All these repressed desires, these desires which had never before been satisfied were suddenly her reality, and she was overflowing with joy. A joy which had turned into an exacerbated and uncontrollable sexual desire. She was there, standing in this apartment, facing a man who did not even want to know her first name, and she wanted to scream and beg him to finally take her. Her whole body shook, she felt as though she was going to lose control of herself.

He got behind her, pressing his chest against her back, while continuing to play with her breasts. The sensation of his body along her back, his cock pressed against the hollow of her arched back, made her let out a groan of uncontrolled desire. She was panting, trying to resist grinding her firm buttocks against him, as if it were some sort of animal instinct she had to ignore. She begged that he would take her. Still against her back, he slid his hands along her hips, taking the measure of her body, immersing himself in the softness of her skin, his expert fingers. He discovered his new toy. With one hand on her belly, he pinned her against him a little more, as if he wanted her to know that he was getting an erection.

She felt his cock, hard, against her buttocks, and pressed herself against him. Without really being aware of it, she wiggled her little hips against him, until he squeezed her so tightly that she could barely move. She was breathing fast; she wanted him so badly. Nothing else mattered to her. She would have given anything for him to finally fuck her, to relieve herself of this violent desire that had seized her. He ran his free hand between her legs, feeling her already soaked pussy. Her body reacted to his touch, she was horny, desperate to have him. She was almost ashamed of it, and yet she had lost all willpower and no longer resisted this flow of sensations. She moaned, enjoying the moment, drunk to feel his hand on her, in her. His hand. His fingers slowly slipped into her tight hole. Then he stopped, suddenly, and moved away.

"That's enough. You are here to satisfy me, not the other way around. And I want to make you wait a little. I'm also the master of your pleasure; remember that, little Slave."

Apollonia lowered her head a little, ashamed of herself, like a horny little bitch in heat, as if he were at her service. She swallowed her saliva and tried to regulate her breathing. This sudden frustration was almost physically painful, and she wondered if she was going to stand waiting over and over, how she was going to manage to contain this powerful drive which she had never felt before.

"On all fours."

The order seemed to come from nowhere. He had snapped his fingers, and pointed to the ground, indicating where he wanted her to be. Apollonia hastened to obey; her breath was short. She remained motionless, silent. The atmosphere was almost oppressive. She stayed frozen for what seemed like a very long time. Her mind was filled with thoughts of desire. She heard him move around her. She did not see him, but just to hear him was more real than the shadow he had been before. He had a voice, a face, a body … a cock. Apollonia bit her lip; she was beginning to realize that she was obsessed with him to the point that it almost scared her. Then the whip hit her hard again.

"Spread your legs." Apollonia obeyed, ashamed of her awkwardness, when another blow slapped her buttocks. Hard.

"I told you to always stay arched."

"Sorry …" She dug her back, offering her rump as much as she possibly could in this position. Thighs wide apart, back arched, she was shameless, totally indecent. Never before had she offered herself like this to a man. To take this position in a dimly lit room during intercourse was one thing, but to expose herself like this, without even being touched, facing someone she had never even seen naked, was far from her norm. He kept circling her body, inspecting it. He walked slowly, calmly, sometimes caressing her curves with the end of his whip. Then he spanked her again. Intimately this time, with the order for her to lower her head. He leaned over her, stroking her tits again, then her buttocks. He lingered again on her pussy, which he finally discovered for the first time, as she waved it in his face, offering it to him. She felt his eyes, his fingers that expertly examined her pussy. She felt ashamed to be so excited by this inspection, an inspection from a man who she did not really know at all.

He slid his fingers between her lips that were swollen with desire, and he penetrated with two fingers, gently at first, then more brutally. She inhaled, hearing the liquid squelch of her pussy as his fingers played with her. She felt more ashamed, but she wanted more too. She moaned, naked and on all fours, under the spell of his fingers, the fingers of the man who owned her. He could demand anything from her, and at that precise moment she was convinced that she had made the correct decision. She wanted nothing else but to be in this position.

His movements became more and more effective and more precise, as if he wanted to discover what affected her the most, the points of her intimate anatomy that reacted best to his expert touch. He was taking his time squatting behind, watching, analyzing this woman who gave herself to him like an animal, her round offered to him without any second thought. She was dripping with desire all over his fingers, moaning and trembling with need.

"Elbows on the ground." Apollonia moved without a

second of hesitation. She still had not acquired the perfect reflex of obedience, and no doubt he had picked up that this was a fault. Apollonia was out of breath, almost unable to believe the reality that she was now in. She mechanically laid her elbows on the ground, offering herself more to him. She fought not to round her back for a moment as his fingers were withdrawn, a little too quickly for her liking. Her normal breathing pattern gently resumed as she watched him move, straightening up on his knees. She wondered what she had done wrong.

"Did I tell you to move?"

"No, Master, sorry … I …"

"Take your position, at once!" She no longer felt the pleasant touch of his fingers on her, but now she just felt indecent, her ass offered to him, her pussy spread and unused. Her heart pounded, not because of her indecency, but because of the intonation of his voice. He was unhappy. His voice was hard, firm, and without any appeal. A voice of a Master. Her Master. She took the exact same position, spreading her legs exactly as before, arching her back to the same degree. She placed her forehead flat on the ground and lay there, waiting.

"Your position is correct, but you have a lot to learn." She felt the whip against her buttocks and thighs about a dozen times. It was not unbearable, but all the same it was far from painless.

"When I tell you a position, you do not change it until I tell you to. You do not know my preferred positions just yet. This is normal, you will learn them with time. But remember that I do not like to repeat myself."

"I will remember, Master."

54

"I should hope so. Stay in that position."

"Yes, Master." Apollonia felt him move away as the pain from her whipping slowly faded. She stayed in that position, completely immobile, silent in a mixture of shame and deep satisfaction. She liked this feeling of restraint, this obligation to immodesty. She loved to feel his power, his obvious authority over her. She was his, and she let this thought sink in. She could not help but smile, sighing a little.

Master Vincent left her for a good ten minutes, which may not have seemed like much, but in these circumstances, it seemed like it was endless for Apollonia. He came and went during this time without her being able to see what he was doing. She was an object. She was a toy that he had left there. He wanted to do something else, and he would return when his desire to play with her came back. She knew this, and instead of being humiliated or irritated, she felt the opposite—happy and full of delight to be treated in this way. Had she not fantasized about this kind of scene during the previous months? Had she not envied all those submissives in his blog who were in the same position as she was in now? Now it was she who was here. She who lived at the feet of this coveted Master, living her dream. She savored this moment, and thought about how much she valued her current position.

Finally, she felt him approaching her. She barely raised her head and saw the toes of his shoes, right in front of her.

"Prostrate yourself." This time, without a second of hesitation, Apollonia tensed, unfolding her arms to lay at either side of him, her forehead between his two feet. She exaggerated her camber to press her breasts against the floor, and intensely savored the few moments he allowed her to stay that way.

"You decided to offer yourself to me, for reasons that I do not know. I will be your Master, and you will serve me without any complacency. I can be very hard sometimes. I'll push you to the extremes, you will exceed your limits. I will be insensitive to your cries and your tears. I will never be sorry for you, because you chose this fate. I'm going to ask you a question, and I'll ask you again in a week. Think about what you're going to say to me, there's no shame to back off, but answer in full consciousness. Do you still want to belong to me and serve me, like a slave?"

"Yes, Master, more than anything."

"On your knees, hands behind your back." Apollonia obeyed; she saw that he was holding a chain which was maybe two feet long.

"I accept you today as a slave, on trial. This first week will be symbolized by this chain that you will wear around your throat at all times, and it is there to remind you of your condition. If we continue, I will offer you a leather collar for the next month. And if you still stay, I'll have to forge you a steel necklace." Apollonia did not answer, the emotions inside her were too strong. She felt him wrap the chain around her neck and lock it with a padlock.

"I'll take it off in seven days, then you'll make your decision. If I want to keep you, it will be necessary to prove yourself here."

"Yes, Master, thank you, Master." Apollonia felt her voice tremble, and without thinking, she prostrated herself again at his feet, without realizing that he had not given the order. He did not, however, stop her from doing so, leaving her to contain her emotion and soak up this moment she had hoped for. He knew it was important to her, and that these minutes were precious to her. For him too, it was not trivial. It was never trivial. He watched her from above, the woman who had flung herself at his feet, trembling. At that moment, he did not see a sex object, he did not see a begging maid, he did not see the shapely body that he would use. At that moment, he saw her pure soul. Sincere. He saw her desire to belong and self-sacrifice. He saw the greatness of the gift she was giving him. Her life. No more, no less. And a shiver ran through his body.

"Get up now."

"Yes, Master." He brought her into the kitchen and gave her a bit more information about the layout of the room, as well as what she would be doing for him. Then he ordered her to make him a coffee, precisely as he loved it, and to serve it on a specific tray.

"It will always be like this when I ask you for a coffee. Always remember the tray and bow to me as I drink it." Apollonia found herself alone in this rather small kitchen, but she already guessed that it would become her refuge, when sometimes he would be hard on her. She liked those few moments when she could move without having his eyes on her, she was free for a little while. But she hastened to join him, with the silver tray in her hands. She saw him sitting on the couch, and without looking up at him, she approached, knelt down, and stretched the tray toward him, humbly. She had not held it close enough to him, and she was duly punished with a small whip to her thigh. She winced.

He left her there, taking a sip of the coffee from time to time, then placing it back on the platter which she carried, as if she were a table. He did not look at her and flipped through a magazine, as anyone would, to relax as he enjoyed his coffee. Apollonia was enjoying this moment. She was smiling. She thought how she would do this over and over again, and it made her happy. Even though she knew that the normal, average woman would have been completely against this, and although it was completely different from anything any other woman would have done during her day, she loved it. She was serene. She had decided not to judge herself anymore, and not to feel guilty anymore. She was not like everyone else. Her desires were certainly different. And so what? She did not disturb anyone. She did not train anyone in her deviance. It would not regress the progress of feminism if she wanted to be like this, if she wanted to submit. Her acts were her own, consistent with her desires, meeting her own needs.

It was her life and she chose to do what she wanted. And what she wanted was to be his. Apollonia suppressed this hint of good morality and focused on her position and her humble attitude. Yes, this scene would made feminists scream, but she was willing and sane, and in the home of Master Vincent, there was no one to judge her. She smiled a little more, just happy to be there, at the feet of her Master.

He made her get up and put away the tray. And when that was done, he told her where she should wait when he would not need her. There was no relaxing on the sofa whilst awaiting an order. She would wait for his orders while kneeling next to the fireplace. There and not anywhere else, even if this meant spending hours at a time there if need be. This prospect did not really attract Apollonia, who was already uncomfortable after a few minutes of kneeling there. It was one of the disadvantages of wanting to be constrained. So, she stayed a few long minutes, knowing that this would be her place for the most part of the day. And then he came back and handed her a pair of fishnet stockings.

"Take off your stockings and put these ones on."

"Yes, Master." That done, he gave her a little maid's apron of white satin and lace.

"You will have several outfits, depending on what you do. For the household, I want you to wear this. Fishnet stockings and a white apron. When I order you to clean up, you will start off by dressing yourself like this in the bathroom."

"Yes, Master."

"I imagine you'll manage, you'll find what you need in the kitchen."

"Yes, Master." He placed a ball gag in her mouth, so she could not speak. She had read about this exact gag in Master Vincent's blog, as well as some other toys he had around his house. It was no longer words or images. She was the one wearing that gag. The ball, big as a golf ball, forced her to keep her jaw open, which didn't allow her to swallow saliva, and the leather strap was very painful along her cheeks. She gradually began to feel that she was no longer in a story; the sensations she felt were totally real.

Apollonia spent the next hour doing the housework. She discovered every square inch of his apartment. This place which was a temple of submission, the home of all her fantasies. The theater in which all the stories she heard had taken place, the stories which she had dissected, word for word, trying to imagine the walls which now surrounded her. This time she was there and had plenty of time to observe and to immerse herself in his home. She cleaned it as if it were a sacred place. She felt infinitely privileged to be there, to discover his business, his privacy.

She did not really feel worthy of it all. She had done nothing to deserve this, to be worthy of the trust he gave her to search through his cupboards. This troubled her a little. She saw him as a demi-god, and yet it had been so easy to break into his life, to feel his fingers on her, to discover everything he owned. She was a little puzzled by all this, even if she did treat each object as if it were precious.

She did notice one thing above all else as she moved her way through his household. It was the constraint of the gag; the pain became ubiquitous, and she found herself cleaning up her saliva, which dripped onto the ground, more than anything else in the house. Getting here may not have been very complicated but staying there would be. And she wanted to prove that she deserved her place. Every moment she was here she wanted to prove herself. To satisfy him, day after day, by being constantly present, knowing how to arouse him and show herself as indispensable, that was her real challenge.

When she thought she had completed her task correctly, she kneeled next to the fireplace while he had settled at the dining room table, with his computer. He did not even acknowledge her for a few minutes, but then approached her, coming right up to her. He was extremely close. He dominated her with all his being. Apollonia fully felt his charisma in his words, and she tilted her head. She felt him manipulate her chain and understood that he was attaching a leash. He ordered her to get on all fours, and she had to walk like that, like a bitch, for the first time in her life, as she was walked around, made to inspect her afternoon's work. As soon as he found something that was not done perfectly she would receive one or several whips.

He explained to her that she should learn so that it was always perfect. Being a slave meant taking pride in all work, even if it was just small. He threatened her with making her lick the toilet bowl clean to underline the importance of her household chores. Apollonia could not acquiesce, still gagged. He emphasized this importance with many hard whips to her back and legs. He explained that it would take time for her to learn to walk well, without ever having to be reminded how to do so. He told her he wanted her to work automatically, so her movements became well-acquired reflexes. This was not to be role play, it would be her true nature. Master Vincent finally released her from her gag and allowed her to go to the bathroom. He explained to her that every time she would do the housework she should go to shower and she could wash herself without having to ask permission; this was one of his rules. After a quick shower, she should get ready, put on her new stockings and whatever new outfit he had left for her. Apollonia inhaled, savoring the hot water which rolled down her body. She took the opportunity to calm down, to get accustomed to her new home, before returning to her spot beside the fireplace. He allowed her to eat, alone, in the kitchen. He then brought her to the entrance of the house and padlocked her to a radiator near the front door. Apollonia watched him take a coat and leave without saying a word. He did give her a small pat on the head, however, as he would have done with a dog. He was going to have lunch.

When he was not there, time seemed to go on forever. She did not know how long she had been waiting or how long she had to wait. She had tried to see if she could get rid of her chain, just to see, but it was impossible. She really felt like a captive. This was not a game. Definitely not. She was his, and she felt it—it was a delicious sensation of oppression, of a little anxiety and claustrophobia, but also of belonging. Apollonia ended up sitting on the floor, her head leaned against the wall, dozing off until she was awakened by a noise at the door. She immediately resumed her kneeling position and waited eagerly for his arrival.

†

Master Vincent came in, followed by Diane. Apollonia had tried to prepare for that, she knew from the beginning that she would be there at some point, but she did not expect it to happen so soon. He took off the padlock and ordered her to get up and put away their coats. He explained that this was her role as a slave, and that would always be the case when he came in from the outside. She nodded and obeyed, without looking up at Diane. When she was done, they had already gone to the living room, and he called for her to make them coffee, just as she did that morning, but to add sugar to Diane's cup.

This situation was very complex, and it felt heavy on her. Apollonia did not know what Diana had thought of her initiative. She seemed angry with her for having offered herself to her Master. Yes, some subjects had a degree of self-sacrifice sufficient to feel no jealousy, threat, or rivalry toward another subject, but it was obvious that it must have been very rare. She was certain that Diane would not at all be her ally. Yet she did not consider herself a competitor, as they were not. Master Vincent had made it clear: Apollonia would never be her equal; Diane would have rights over her. Hierarchically speaking, Apollonia was less than Diane. And Apollonia was going to find out how much. She stepped forward, head down, still not meeting the eyes of Diane, and knelt down in front of Master Vincent who had sat on the couch. Diane was also kneeling beside him, but to his side, her head lying on his thigh, her face turned toward him. Apollonia stood motionless, gently tending the tray to her Master before lowering her head a little bit. He grabbed the tray and ordered her to go on all fours, aside. She did it, blushing, alongside him, her head to the side of Diane. He asked her to keep her back flat and he placed the tray on it. Diane had straightened up, and naturally, as she would have done in front of a coffee table, she went to settle in front of her Master, on the other side of this table made of flesh, and began to mix the sugar into her coffee.

"What do you think of my slave?"

"She is beautiful, and very docile apparently, Master."

It was the first time Apollonia had heard the sound of her voice. She felt no animosity, no rancor, but she knew that that could be feigned. Yet she quickly felt a hand caress her buttocks, with a feminine delicacy. She remained as still as possible, but internally she was troubled. Disturbed by what she would have to do with this woman, or another, for that matter. By offering herself to Master Vincent, she knew that he would have the right to lend her to others, and that she should submit. She knew she should have sex with anyone Master Vincent would choose, even if they were strange, vulgar, or violent. He had all rights over her. Even that one. She knew this. It would happen, at some point, and she would have to obey. She was not ready for it, not just yet. She had only been there for a few hours, and she found herself naked, on all fours, and a woman she had never spoken to was caressing her buttocks.

These caresses were, however, very ephemeral. Diane spoke with Master Vincent as if they were alone, and even though it was difficult for Apollonia to be sure of it, she spoke with such confidence, she was sure. Despite the particularly humiliating situation in which she was in, she did not really feel ashamed or belittled. She was not responsible for her position, she was just obeying. Yes, the situation she was in was open to criticism, but it was down to her owner to complain, not her. She was not responsible for a single thing. She had to let him guide her, control her in every aspect. But it was not just the desire to do, it was the fact of being made to do so which is what excited her. What she liked was being ordered, the obligation to obey, this feeling of never being able to say no to him whatever his demands were, because he was the Master. Her Master.

Apollonia did not miss a beat of their conversation, even

if it was not the most exciting. She drank in their words, she got drunk at the sound of their voices. Despite the pain she felt from being in this position, she did not really want this moment to end, she felt good. After a while, Master Vincent made her return to the kitchen to tidy up and return to her place, near the fireplace. He handed her the ball gag, a blindfold for her eyes, and she was forced to keep her hands on her head. Not just behind the neck, but actually atop her head. He widened the gap between her thighs and checked the arch of her back, and then ordered her to stay that way. He went away, and the other orders she heard were not for her, but rather for Diane. Apollonia did not see anything, she simply listened. Just the sound of movement, a belt being undone, accelerated breathing, an open mouth begging to be filled. Diane, a few meters away from her, sucked her Master. Blind and dumb, Apollonia's throat tightened, and she felt uneasy.

Then, little by little, the breathing of Diane, her little moans of pleasure, started to sexually arouse her. She was so eager to take her place, discover his cock, to taste it, finally. Her breath began to become quicker. She was horny. The position imposed on her became a torture, and she began to doubt that he would intend to involve her in one way or another. Other noises, other positions, other moans. He penetrated. Right there, in front of her blind eyes, he was in the process of fucking Diane, who did not hide her pleasure. And then his words. For her. For Diane. For a moment, Apollonia felt like before, invisible behind her screen, non-existent.

It was as if nothing had changed, she did not count. She was not really there. The excitement and the desire left her immediately, and she was left alone. She felt as if they were not truly there, and not because of her blindfold. She tried to isolate herself internally. What had she thought? That it was enough to proclaim herself his slave and deserve all the attention? That this title would have given her some privileges, without even having to deserve them? That her presence would make him renounce others, and his habits? The evidence pained her. By becoming a slave, she did not become the one she had read about in the stories of Master Vincent, as she was still there, and at this moment, he possessed her as much as one can possess somebody.

Apollonia realized that the path would be long and arduous, but she would not give up, certainly not. Her role was that of a slave, not that of a submissive. She was in her place. She had to learn not to think about her own desires, and this was probably the key to understanding all this. The meaning of the abnegation she said she wanted. Apollonia had thought many times about all this; living it made her see things so much more concretely, like seeing through a window finally cleared of fog.

Self-denial was not something that was decided, it had to come from somewhere deeper in herself and above all, it had to be deeply sincere. Apollonia aspired to that, probably more than any other thing. But she understood that it would probably be more complicated than she had thought. Master Vincent used raw words to which Diane seemed particularly receptive. She shouted without real restraint under his thrusts, and even plunged into darkness, Apollonia could imagine the scene perfectly. She guessed where they were, there, just in front of her. Just on the other side of the darkness, as before on the other side of the screen. They eventually went away, no doubt to go to another room, maybe his room or the bathroom. Apollonia lay there, guessing what was happening elsewhere, but not daring leave her position.

When they came back, Master Vincent rescued her from her blindfold. He no longer wore his clothes from before, but just black trousers. He was shirtless and realizing it,

Apollonia could not help but to stare, admiringly. She would be greedy, as if it were the only occasion that she would have to see his body. Her eyes were slipping from his shoulders to the bottom of his back, drooling over his muscular torso. She imagined him sliding his hands over her, his tongue, and desire came back all too quick. Diane herself had dressed and was already ready to leave.

"Slave! The coat of my submissive."

Apollonia hastened to obey, even more relieved to leave this position than hearing of Diane's departure. She took the coat and helped her put it on, head down, fully in her role of slave. She felt the look of her Master, who was looking for a fault. But Apollonia made sure she did everything correctly, especially in front of Diane.

†

Once Diane left, Master Vincent brought Apollonia to the couch. She remained on her knees, the ball gag still between her teeth.

"I appreciate your behavior. I'm starting to believe that you know what submission and obedience represents. Some already experienced submissives are not as disciplined." Apollonia could not speak, but she heard his words. They were for her, just for her. She dared to look up to him, and this exchange of a glance, at that moment, was worth more than any words. She existed for him. She too had gone from a shadow to reality.

"I'm proud of you. For the moment. I had contemplated sending you back before the end of the day, but I'm curious. You will continue to serve me. I will not trap you. I will not be too hard to make you give up. I will be as I am. Demanding, severe, but always right." Apollonia nodded, stars in her eyes; if she had spoken, she might have burst into tears. Her emotions were much too much strong and intense. She liked that. She liked to feel these unique sensations, of another world. Indescribable.

"Prostrate before your Lord and Master." Apollonia hastened to obey. It was as if he had read her thoughts; she had prayed that he would allow her to do that. This was a sign of the link that was born between a Master and his slave. This link she had heard so often in the blogs she consulted, eager to know. She remained there for a long time, trembling intensely. He undid the strap of the ball gag and released her mouth.

"Listen carefully to your instructions, I will not repeat them. You'll go and run me a bath, making sure that the temperature is ideal—hot, but not too hot. You will add foam. When it is ready, you will come to me, you will beg at my feet and tell me. Is this understood?"

"Yes, Master."

"Go."

Apollonia stood up, and went away to the bathroom adjoining his room, since the others only had a shower. She respected her instructions and came to announce that his bath was ready. Once in the bathroom, he ordered her to undress him. On her knees, she complied, almost uncomfortable with so much intimacy, finally revealing the naked body of her Master. She scarcely dared to look at him. He slipped into the water, and thus remained a long time, before ordering her to go and get him a glass of wine. She would find a bottle of Pinot Gris in the kitchen. She brought it, on the tray, and knelt beside the tub. He observed her, and he was satisfied.

"Your role will often boil down to this, do you realize?"

"It is the role of a slave to serve their Master."

"What made you want to live in these conditions?"

"You, Master ... well, I think it was always in me, but it became obvious after reading your blog."

"You may be disappointed."

"I do not believe so, Teacher."

"We will see ..."

He took a long break. And Apollonia did not dare take the initiative of the conversation. No doubt he wanted to give her time to realize the possibility that everything might not happen as she dreamed. For him too, finally, the pressure was strong enough. He had not asked for anything, he had warned her. But he knew that he would feel bad if in a few days she decided to leave, bitter and deeply disappointed with him, and this slave condition forever denatured.

Yet, when he watched her, head down, a few red curls falling here and there around her face, he could not refrain from thinking too that she seemed in her place.

"I will never use you sexually in the presence of Diane. But the opposite will happen, as you may have realized. I do not always cover your eyes. Sometimes I will send you to another room, to stay alone with her."

"Yes, Master."

"Have you ever had sex with a woman?"

"No, Master."

"Do you want to?"

Apollonia paused. Not only did she not know if she wanted to or not, but she did not really understand why he asked her opinion. Would he not decide for her?

"I do not really know, Master …" Her voice had become weaker, and she repeated to herself in her head: Do not take my desires into account …

"Diane likes me to lend her my other submissive. But I like the idea of your status being different. I will see."

"Yes, Master."

Gradually, she dared to raise her eyes even more to see a little bit of him, a fragment of his amber skin covered with foam. Immediately, her desire warmed her stomach. His glass finished, he then explained to her how he demanded she behave if he did not give her the order to wash him. She had to take the bath towel, get on her knees, and put the folded towel in her forearms, all in a humble posture. She had to wait for him to come out in that position, without saying anything. When he came out of the bath, she should show him the bath towel, arms outstretched. Afterwards, she could dry his body. The ritual would always be the same.

Apollonia flinched at this idea. Impatient to deserve such an honor. She understood that all of this would come with time, she had to wait. She had to prove the sincerity of her commitment. One day, maybe, all this would become perfectly natural; he would have to say nothing, a look, a gesture, and she would know what to do. He went out and dried himself, then knotted the towel around his waist. Apollonia was staring at him; she liked the way he moved, and she could finally smell his scent in her nose. She watched his body.

Suddenly, he pulled his hair back, raised his head, and looked at her. She was terrified at the thought to have committed a mistake, already ready to beg forgiveness, without even knowing what she had done wrong.

"What were you thinking about right now? Do not lie to me."

"I ... I ..."

"Answer! If you are honest, you have nothing to fear."

"I thought ... that I want you ..." He released his towel slowly and smiled.

"Are you here to satisfy cravings?"

"No, Master, I'm here to satisfy yours ... excuse me ..."

"At least your answer was sincere. Do not lie to me. Ever. You understand?"

"Yes, Master."

Apollonia was still out of breath. He suddenly grabbed the back of her head with such force she believed that she was about to be punished. Master Vincent stood in front of her. Upright, dominant, sure of himself.

"Do you want to suck your Master?"

"Yes, Master."

"Go ahead and show me everything you know."

Apollonia gasped. She wanted to make this last forever, not for his pleasure, but for her own. She had wanted to do this ever since she'd read his blog. And now she was able to.

She raised her hands to his hips. On her knees, she had her face just in front of his cock. He was becoming erect, and that made her smile. She moaned with excitement, slowly opening her mouth, surrounding his cock with her lips without yet touching it. And then finally, as the culmination of all her fantasies, she licked slowly, up and down, wrapping her tongue all around, groaning. She thought of Diane, who did the same thing a few hours ago. She hoped to suck him the way he liked it. This thought had never crossed her mind before with the lovers she had had in the past, and she knew that she could please them easily. But he was not a man like others. He was her Lord and Master. His standards would be higher, he could not settle for something "okay" or "correct." He was going to demand excellence. It was necessary that she give the best of herself. And more.

He let go of her, watching her suckle on his erect penis. He felt her lips, her tongue. He felt the moisture of her mouth, its warmth. His breathing became faster. He could see his chest rising and falling rapidly, and Apollonia could tell that he wanted her. He wanted nothing more than to bend her over, his hands on her hips, and to fuck her. But he was patient, he wanted to wait. He wanted her to wait. He liked seeing her bend to his desire and begging for him. He wanted to see her at the end of her breath, losing control. He let her suck him for a long time. He had mastered his body to perfection and knew what to do to contain his pleasure. He would have his fun when he wanted to, when he would be done with her. He wanted to play first.

"Go to the living room, on all fours."

"Yes, Master." Apollonia obeyed. She took the order without thinking. She had sucked it. She had tasted Master Vincent's cock in her mouth; this Master whom she had been worshiping for months had granted her this favor.

"Fuck your Master's feet, Slave." She hastened to obey and reveled in his demand, a demand which she had fantasized about countless times. She did it with such vigor and passion that Master Vincent smiled at her. She was going to be a good slave, obviously.

"That's enough. Lie on your back." She complied, not thinking about what was to come next; she was living in the present moment, everything else was abstract. She was in another world, in a kind of strange bubble of well-being. And she liked that. She enjoyed this madness.

A few whips to her buttocks made her understand that she had to spread her thighs further. She found herself lying down, facing him standing between her legs. He dominated her with his whole being. She was out of breath, trembling with desire. She felt her indecency and that excited her even more; she wriggled gently without even being aware of it.

"Caress yourself. But do not enjoy yourself. I forbid it." Apollonia swallowed. She had this second of floating, this second during which her mind and body contradicted each other at the thought of his order, seeking a way to escape it, and then submit to it and surrender. Whatever he asked for, she had to obey. Then she slid her middle finger onto her clit and shivered immediately as she was already sensitive. She was wet, slippery. She was trying not to moan but she could not manage to stop herself. He whipped her again. She closed her eyes, too embarrassed to look at him. The whip still slapped with an audible crack, and she opened her legs as wide as possible.

Never had she offered herself as such to a man. It was as if she were back in her studio, when she was having fun after reading Master Vincent's blog. Now she was facing him. Immodest. Her moans were accelerating, she could not take it anymore. She had to slow down the movements of her finger to calm down just a little. Her mind became more lucid and she regained consciousness of her position, of his gaze on her, and the excitement returned immediately. He ordered her to continue, and not to stop under any pretext. And, most importantly, not to enjoy herself. She felt him move away and became ashamed of herself, thinking she had done something wrong. However, he returned shortly after with a sex toy which he gave her.

"Put it in." She paused for a second, then firmly grabbed the dildo and slid it inside of herself, gasping. She was so soaking wet it slid into her easily, despite its girth. She wanted to continue, but Apollonia did not dare, she did not know what to do. She had stopped fondling herself and was holding the dildo with one hand, without moving, in suspense. She needed an order, she needed his words to dare to continue. Otherwise, it would have been like she acted on her own, and it would not have had the same effect on her. However, no word came from his mouth, but rather the hissing crack of his whip struck between her thighs, where the skin is soft and fragile. Three red streaks stood up from her porcelain skin.

"Keep caressing yourself. I want to see that dildo move. Now! Obey!"

Apollonia complied. It was strangely easier. She was obeying, she had no choice. She offered herself. To act as such before his eyes was something terrible—quite indecent, which made her completely mad with excitement. She writhed with pleasure, every inch of her contorting, so grabbed by the sensations of her body that she did not even think of her indecency; she was elsewhere, in a place she had never known. And then his whip caressing her thighs, and sometimes snapped softly, not to hurt, but just so she did not forget that he was there, watching all her actions, judging her ability to surrender. And his words. She loved his words, the sound of his voice. This intonation that she had so often tried to imagine. He told her that she was very obedient, that he wanted to be able to demand her. That he had all the rights to her. She had to submit. Again, and again. Because he was her Lord and Master.

She was on the verge of begging him to cum, she could not stand it anymore. Her feet were squirming, her hands ran all over her body. She was panting, her back arched. She wanted him to take her there and then. To finally enter her.

"That's enough." She stopped, slowly removing the dildo in a last groan. She was out of breath, sweating, realizing her situation, a little ashamed to have let herself go as much as she did.

"Don't move. Stay as you are until you are told, little slut." With his foot, he spread her legs a little more, and left her there as he fetched a bottle of wine from the pantry. This wait was a torture for Apollonia who felt much more embarrassed to remain so without moving, without his orders nor his presence. She kept her eyes closed and waited for him to come back. But that was not the case, he did not approach her. He settled down in front of his computer and stayed there for a long time. She recovered from her emotions, slowly. Her breathing regained its normal pace. He watched her without her being able to see him. He was looking at her body which she offered, her wild hair, her chest rising and falling, and her quivering legs. He was thinking of making her stay this way for hours, just for his enjoyment. Absolute power, total control over her body, over this slave. There was nothing he enjoyed more than a woman completely submitting herself to him. More than sex. More than being served. He had something within him which made women feel as if they would do anything for him in order to please, despite everything he asked. He could read them, he knew their expectations, their unacknowledged and unfulfilled desires and requests. He took pleasure in seeing her so; so vulnerable, so submissive. He had left his computer and was enjoying his wine while watching her, at the same time happy of this slave who had surrendered herself to him, and conscious of the responsibility that it represented.

After a while, he ordered her to come back to him, and to suck on him again. Apollonia complied quickly, almost throwing herself on his cock. She could not take it anymore. She wanted to do her best for him, but she wanted to make him want her too, just as much as she wanted him. She wanted him to lose control. But she came to realize that he had not just mastered her, but also his desires. He could control himself, and he controlled her. He made her lick his balls, suck them, and then run her tongue up and down the length of his shaft. His requests were precise and she tried to satisfy him as best as possible, hoping to feel his cum deep in her throat as a way of saying thank you. But instead he stopped everything and ordered her to the kitchen to prepare dinner. It was like a cold shower for Apollonia, but she understood that he was going to make her wait to show her his mastery, and to constrain her in her frustration. He was the master of the game and he was playing with her. She had to accept that, and she needed to remain patient. She knew that, sooner or later, he would want her enough to go further.

†

Apollonia followed his instructions and prepared his food as best she could, wearing her maid's apron as she cooked. He ate alone in the living room, in front of the TV, while she had to eat in the kitchen, always attentive in case he needed anything. After his meal, he allowed Apollonia to have some time in the bathroom, so that she could shower. He remained alone in front of the TV, watching a film, and spoke to her without moving his eyes from the screen. She went to the bathroom with her head down, frustrated and disappointed at not having been able to pleasure him more.

She showered, taking her time since he allowed her to do so. She finished, came out of the shower, and instantly froze. Her heart beat in her mouth. The door was closed. Not locked, but closed. She racked her brain, trying to remember if it was she who had closed it. She was not completely certain, but deep inside, she knew that she had shut the door by pure reflex. She did not follow his instructions. Apollonia held her breath and went back to him. Maybe he didn't realize it? She felt her hands tremble, not through fear, but through the anger she felt at herself for slipping up. How could she have forgotten to leave the door open? He had been so clear about it. She knelt at his feet, and without even looking at his face she understood that he knew of her mistake. She lowered her head a little more.

"Why are you here?"

"To serve you and obey you, Master. I ask you, forgive me …"

"Are you able to respect an order?"

"Yes, Master, sorry, I … it was not on purpose … it will not happen again."

"I know. It will not happen again. Remember my words: I do not like to repeat. I tell you once, you're supposed to know. If you make a mistake, you are severely punished.

You make a mistake, you leave. Is this clear?"

"Yes, Master. I'm sorry …"

"I told you to leave the door open. Always leave it open, whatever you do. You belong to me, you are not entitled to any privacy; if I want to come and see you in the shower, or watch you pissing, I'll do it, and I do not have to open a door to do that. I want you to feel this lack of freedom during every second of your day, and just how much I control you. This is why you came to me, no? That's what you told me the first time we met, isn't it? 'I want to belong to you ...' That's what you said, no?"

"Yes, Master, that's what I want ..."

"You have a lot to learn, then. Remember that if I ever ask you to do something, it is because it is within your reach to do so. You are able to do everything I say. Leaving the door open is not exactly complicated, is it?"

"No, Master ..."

"Then you will be punished. Already. I thought you would be able to go through today without slipping up but … I was wrong …" Apollonia bowed her head a little more, ashamed of idiotic forgetfulness. What she was asked to do was not difficult. It was just her forgetfulness, and it was extremely difficult for her, mentally, to face that. She was already disappointing him. She was not up to standard. She felt tears running down her cheeks, silently.

All the emotions and stress accumulated during the day, all the fatigue of these waiting positions, everything was catching up with her; she felt exhausted. He grabbed her by the hair to drag her into the middle of the room, and ordered her to take up the prostrate position, her breasts on the floor, thighs apart, but hands alongside her body. He tied her wrists to her ankles; she found herself completely unable to move. Her cheek rested against the hard, wooden floor. He left her there for a few minutes, and then he asked her how many whips she deserved for her error.

"I ... I do not know, Master, only you know ..." she whispered.

"If I ask you your opinion, you give it to me! It's not up to you to judge whether I know or not!" Apollonia was taken aback; she thought she had answered well, but she had committed yet another fault.

"Thirty strokes, Master?" Apollonia had noticed during her readings that it was a number that often came back during punishments. And it seemed to work, as Master Vincent began to whip her. This time, the blows were more forceful. More than those she had received to correct her position. She had a hard time trying not to flinch. She bit her tongue, trying not to let out a loud cry, but she could not suppress a few stifled groans of pain. She had counted each stroke in her head, to know when it was going to end.

"I think you have the abilities to be a good slave. I will educate you so that you serve me better. I'll train you, as you train an animal, until you become the obedient dog that I want you to be. I do not want you if you are constantly imperfect, if I must correct you at every moment. If you do not feel up to it, your freedom to quit and leave is the only freedom you have. The only. If you stay, you willingly submit yourself to me. You obey. And you spend all your time, all your thoughts, all your actions on me. Understood?"

"Yes, Master."

"Do you want to go home?"

"No, Master."

Master Vincent smiled, satisfied. "Tonight, you will think about your condition. On this life that you have chosen. I'm not going to give you pleasure, you're at fault. You will not sleep at the foot of my bed, it's something that needs to be deserved. I'm going to put your bitch cushion in the hallway, and you will sleep chained."

"Yes, Master …"

"I told you. No special treatment. No compassion. You came for yourself. You must accept your decision."

"I do not regret my decision, Master. I regret that I have disappointed you …"

"You'll learn. It's up to you that it does not happen again." He untied her and dragged her into the hall, chaining her neck. He threw a blanket at her and left. She curled up on her cushion and began to cry. Yet as she wept, the clatter of his chain made her smile. Everything was so complex and contradictory. The path she had chosen would be hard and difficult, but she was more convinced than ever that it was what she wanted. She wanted more than anything to please him and to satisfy. Apollonia slept badly that night. Yet she had often dreamed of this chain and this bitch cushion. But this life was so new and overwhelming. Even in knowing what to expect, having read it, studied it, nothing equaled the reality.

†

She woke up feeling her Master gently shake her shoulder. She opened her eyes, realized that it was not a dream, and smiled at him. He had explained to her how she should greet him in the morning.

Apollonia sat up and kissed each of his shoes, as he had ordered, as her morning ritual. Still on her knees, she kissed the palm of his hand and was then allowed to greet him. He answered softly, "Hello, Slave." These two words, this situation reflecting her condition in his simple expression, made her deeply happy. The morning passed without much particularity. He prepared breakfast for them both, and she ate alone in the kitchen. Then she performed the household chores, without failing to put on the stockings and apron which he had provided. When she was done, he inspected her work, much like the day before. Apollonia realized that it would always be so, even though sometimes his inspections would become less systematic, and random. He did not complain much, and he congratulated her on her work. It allowed her, little by little, to forget what had happened the day before, or at least, to accept that it had happened, and all she had to do was not make the same mistake again.

Moreover, after her chores, she had to go shower, and this time she did not forget to leave the door open. She sensed that she would never again commit that fault, and that kind of habitual reflex for anyone, like closing the door to go to the toilet when one is not alone, would soon be part of a distant past. When she returned, she settled where she should, near the fireplace. He then made her come and stand in front of him. He stared at her for a long time, turning her around, his hands on her head. Then he began to caress her, first gently, then more brutally. She was already in perfect condition—hot and moist. She was moaning at the slightest touch of his fingers. How long had it been since she last had sex? Eight months? Ten months? She did not know anymore. She could not take it anymore.

He slid his fingers deep inside her, feeling her letting herself go and surrender, then he stroked her clit until she lost all control. Consciously or not, she had started to move on him, to feel it even more, she begged him internally. Then, finally, he bent her over the glass table, her breasts pressed against the cool, hard surface, and grabbed her wrists with one of his hands. He did not have to ask her to spread her legs; on the contrary, she offered herself as much as she possibly could. She felt his cock sink into her all the way, then slide in and out quickly, and she savored every sensation like never before. She moaned, she gasped, moving her ass as much as possible to encourage him to go faster, to fuck her deeper.

He let go of her wrists and clung to her hips, unceremoniously, without any delicacy. He took to her with brutality, animality, and she would not have liked it to be any other way. She began to scream with pleasure, her chain clinking against the glass of the table, to the rhythm of his thrusts, but nothing distracted him as he used his slave in a way in which he deemed fit. He owned her. She was his toy. And she liked that.

He grabbed her by the hair and turned her round, making her kneel in front of him. He held her head in his hands, and used her mouth as he had used her pussy. He penetrated her again, always brutally, kneading her breasts and pinching her nipples. He sometimes forced her to raise her head, pulling her by the hair. He told her how she was unneeded, that she was just a sex object, that she was nothing, just a toy he used for his pleasure. She wanted to hear it again and again. She wanted him to degrade her, to humiliate her with his words.

She sometimes answered a "Yes, Master" between two moans. She would have liked to tell him what she was for him, but she did not dare. He returned to her mouth, and although he did not physically pleasure her, her excitement was so strong that she moaned again. She savored feeling his dick in her mouth, thinking that he was going to cum in her, to honor her of his enjoyment. When he came, she felt like she had too, as he shot a hot, sticky load into her mouth. She swallowed it and gently continued to suck until he pulled back. She caught her breath, slowly, while kneeling, head down. He slid his hand down her cheek and urged her to lift her eyes to him. He smiled at her and spoke softly.

"Thanks, Slave."

"Oh, it's me who thanks you, Master ..." Apollonia immediately dropped her eyes, almost embarrassed. It was her role to give him pleasure, not the other way around. He insisted with his hand that she look at him again. As she shyly looked up at him, he leaned over her and laid a kiss on her forehead. Then he left.

Apollonia stayed alone on her knees in the middle of the living room; she still had the taste of his cum in her mouth. She felt the warmth of his kiss, the softness of his lips on her skin. She had stayed frozen, as if she did not want to move to keep the intensity of this moment intact. She savored this attention, this delicious reward, almost too precious.

She understood that everything she had imagined, all which she had fantasized, was not abstract. The physical sensations she could have imagined, but not the emotions. She liked that he told her that she was nothing when they fucked, but that kiss, that simple gesture showed the opposite, and it was in these small gestures, in those glances, that a bond was created. This precious, invaluable link, which united a Master and his slave. What she aspired to more than anything was to feel total self-denial. She had only been there for twenty-four hours, and she only doubted her abilities, but not her motivation; she felt absolutely certain to have made the right choice. Moments like this would be worth all the suffering and hardship.

The day went a little like the previous one, except that he remained absent for a long time during the afternoon. He had chained her like the day before, but in the bathroom so she could use the toilet if needed. He had also left her the handset of the landline phone with his number, and the strict prohibition to use it for anything other than calling him in the case of extreme urgency. She stayed there, alone, for a few long hours. He explained that it would often be so. That she was a slave and not a companion. She no longer had her own identity, she was no longer a woman, she was a slave. Apollonia liked that, even if she was bored quickly by her surroundings. But she was so busy with her new life, this condition, that she could not have focused on any other activity.

He did not return until the evening, with a takeaway dinner he ate in the living room. She made her own meal and ate it quickly. After this he brought her to his feet.

"How was your day, Slave?"

"Good, Master."

"Do you really think you'll like this life?"

"I'm sure, Master."

"It's not even been two days."

"I can't explain why I know it, but I know, deep inside me. I want this."

"I will not be very present this week, I will work

sometimes here, but also outside. I will often leave you chained. I like to know that you have no freedom when I'm not there."

"Yes, Master. I understand."

"I'll leave you some magazines or a book."

"Yes, Master."

"Tonight again, you'll sleep in the hallway. You did not do anything wrong, but Diane will be here, and she will spend the night with me. No doubt sometimes I will want to have you both, but not this time."

"Yes, Master." Apollonia's throat was tight for a few moments before she regained control of herself. She had to accept that. She owed everything to him. After all, she was there. Closer than ever to him. How long had they been meeting while she was staring at her screen? Why did it seem more difficult now than before, when she was far away and invisible? It was more than she had ever dared hope at the time, when it had been so different.

Diane was there before. Diane was there at that time, and Diane would be there after too. It was so. Apollonia resigned herself. Before, she had nothing of it, now she was living at his home, she was breathing the same air as him, she smelled his perfume to the point of drunkenness, she spent her time kneeling at his feet. She smiled at this idea, and gradually, the fact that the shadow of Diane was going to float constantly around them seemed less important.

Master Vincent allowed her to stay near him while waiting for Diane to arrive. He wanted to know what kind of books she liked to read, probably to know what to give her during his absences. He then asked her to lie down at his feet, and she looked up at him, almost destabilizing him for a moment. He watched her curl up against his shoes, her cheek against one of them, her hand surrounding his ankle, in a perfect stillness that reflected the fear that the slightest movement would cause him to send her away from him. She almost seemed to have stopped breathing, as if to be as discreet and quiet as possible.

For Apollonia, this moment was very symbolic; these gestures were simple, but full of meaning to her, and she had imagined doing this so often. She was fully immersed in her condition, in all these first times. It was important to her to never do anything without feeling the magic. She was always in full awareness that never again would she do that for the first time, and that she had to revel in every second. She was there, her cheek against his foot, like a little bitch who falls asleep slowly, closer to his Master.

†

The sound of the doorbell made her jump. Diane was already there. Apollonia met the eyes of Master Vincent, to make sure what she had to do, but she already knew. She got up and went to open the door. She took Diane's coat and hung it in the closet while she was going to the living room to join their Master. She was always so sublime. Perfectly prepared. Her black dress with almost bluish sheen gave her the appearance of a dancer, and her body fitted it beautifully.

Apollonia watched her move toward him, her step delicious—sexy, swaying, she perfectly mastered the wearing of her disproportionate heels. She exuded grace and incredible assurance. Apollonia lowered her head a little; she felt bland compared to her. She went quietly to her knees at his place, after serving them a drink. She attended their evening, to their games. She listened to their conversation, watched their movements, their looks. She saw her undress and offer herself, she heard his breathing, his sighs, and his moans.

She saw him caressing her buttocks, fingering her pussy. She looked at her to submit, to give herself to him with a feline grace, facilitated by repeated gestures. Diane guessed his expectations, she anticipated his desires. His body was sweating with desire and pleasure, his skin was glistening and looked all the more beautiful and softer. She had animal like flexibility. He forced her, he was hitting her and submitting her with some kind of disturbing delicacy. Even the rawest words, which would have made any other scene obscene, seemed just right and so obvious that they lost their vulgar side. All their actions were fluid and harmonious, yet they did not love: he possessed her body, he used it, he insulted it. He dominated.

Apollonia could not take her eyes off their bodies. She saw him, as he had so often been. His torso, broad and muscular, his gaze when he took her, or when she sucked him. She was seeing herself behind her screen, reading his words before caressing herself, alone in her bed. Tonight, she was facing them, in front of him. Spectator of their session. Unable to define what she felt. She could not have said whether to be a witness of their pleasures excited her, or if on the contrary, she felt ill. She was in another state, indescribable, a mixture of acceptance and jealousy, understanding and suffering, need and renunciation. Everything was mixing, everything was fluctuating and overwhelming.

It came in waves. A wave of sadness to be so relegated— but this thought of being a useless spectator was immediately replaced by a wave of pride to be the slave who was honored by their presence. Then a tidal wave swept it all away, as she would never count as much as Diane, as her own link could not match the one which they had woven. She watched their bodies, filled with pleasure, shining with sweat, their breasts rising again quickly. Their eyes, sometimes closed, sometimes staring intensely at each other, their lips frozen on two smiles which spoke a thousand words.

Apollonia lowered her head. She did not want to see anymore. She had seen too much. She quenched her contradictory thoughts, seeking the balance between doubt and resolutions. She thought back to the kiss that he had put on her forehead, the delicious moment of fullness that she had felt.

This conviction of being able to accept everything for such sensations. She clung to that. She did not want to see or hear them, she was hiding in her bubble to recover and recharge. To remember what had brought her here. She had never doubted that he would impose on her such situations, she had not imagined that she would have a hard time supporting them. She had gone to the other side of the mirror, from fantasy to reality, and it was a lot harder than she thought …

"Slave. Champagne."

The order snapped her back to reality. She raised her head and took a second to understand and react. Then she went to the kitchen to fetch two glasses of champagne and put them on a plate with some macaroons that he had bought in the afternoon. She carried it to them on a silver tray and knelt down to serve them. He ran his hand against her cheek, and she looked up. In this glance, he read in her confusion, her doubts too, perhaps. He understood her confusion, but thought again that she chose this life. She would accept, or she could leave. He ordered her to make use of the bathroom and go to sleep on her cushion, in the entrance, as soon as she was ready. He would tie her chain later. Apollonia complied.

A kind of melancholy had taken hold of her but nothing enough to make her give up. She waited a long time, alone in this hallway where she could not see nor hear what was going on in the living room. She was not worthy of staying close to them. Spectator of their antics, yes, but not their other moments. These were only theirs. It was like before when she realized she could not read everything through his words.

She knew a lot, but the most intimate he kept for himself. Exposing a body, to show his pleasure and his way of dominating, did not seem to pose a problem, on the contrary, but to reveal the rest, the gestures of tenderness, they remained secret. As much for his readers as for his slave. Apollonia restrained herself from sobbing, she had to harden herself. She knew it. One day, no doubt, all this would be a disconcerting banality to her. She could not sleep, images of their bodies danced before her eyes, as if the scene replayed indefinitely. And then, finally, he came to her. He crouched down and gently stroked her hair. She straightened to kneel. Head down.

"Look at me."

Apollonia looked up, nervously. Was he to punish her for her discomfort earlier? "You did well today, and tonight you were perfect. You'll be a good slave, I think. I'm proud of you."

Apollonia let out a few tears. She buried her face in his hand which caressed her cheek, and she thanked him. He stayed like that, letting her evacuate this overflow of emotion.

"Tomorrow, you will sleep near your Lord and Master, you deserved it."

"Thank you, Teacher."

"The path you have chosen is difficult. Very difficult. I will not make it easy, you know that. I do not have to adapt."

"I know, Master, I accept it."

"I will push you far in your condition. I want you to accept every request."

"Yes, Master, I will learn, and I will succeed."

"We will see." He looked at her for a moment and smiled at her; she had swallowed her tears and lowered her head again. "Good night, Slave."

"Thank you, Master, you too."

He stood up and forced her to kiss each of his feet and to wish him a good night. It would be like this every night. Apollonia obeyed without hiding her pleasure in this little evening ritual. She tried to make the moment last and touch her lips on his bare skin, but he pulled back and walked away. He walked by again a few minutes later to go to his room, accompanied by Diane who was not dressed. Apollonia rolled herself into a ball and buried her head in her cushion, half sulky, half happy.

†

The days of the week passed. Apollonia had found her pace and was accustomed to all those rituals that accompanied every task, every moment. Master Vincent did not allow her to come and go when he was not there, and she often stayed chained, as she read or rested. But usually, she spent her time thinking about her place in her Master's world, to this choice of life, probably unjustifiable to anyone. She liked being there, she felt good, and the fact that no one could really understand it was not a valid argument to deprive oneself of it. She was preparing the meals for her Master, when he was there, she did the housework, she served him at every moment, it was constantly available.

She was learning fast. He did not take advantage of her body as often as she wanted, but whenever he did, she savored every second and gave her body and soul to him, to please him. He used her according to his desires; she began to know his desires and what he liked: the precise positions he wanted her in each had a name that she had to remember so that she could execute each one immediately.

There were dozens. There were ones he loved, classics, like on all fours, or more indecent, like where she had to lay on her back, legs widely apart and raised, knees almost touching her shoulders. He called it the position of offering. Sometimes he made her do it just to humiliate her, to remind her of what she was, and then he left her thus, in the middle of the room. He did not touch her and did not really look at her either. At least she did not see him, but she knew that he watched her. But he loved to look at her. Beyond the sexual aspect, it was her extreme submission that he loved, her need to obey, without ever sighing or fidgeting. So sometimes he approached, and caressed her, using her as an object. She was excited every time this happened, even in the expectation, being relegated to the rank of a decorative object. It was indeed this slave condition that excited her, even more than the sex.

She moaned very quickly, immediately receptive. He slid his fingers in her and on her clit until the orgasm quickly came after a few seconds. And then he went away. She quickly realized that she should not leave her position, after a strong punishment the first time she had committed that fault.

Diane did not come that week, but he was often away during the day, and she imagined that he was with her. But when her Master came home, he woke her up without hesitation, and ordered her to take his coat and his shoes, sometimes just for that, sometimes also for one last drink. Apollonia loved those times when he pulled her out of her sleep in the middle of the night to demand something from her. She felt like his slave. He never allowed her to share his bed during this week of testing, but she could sleep at the bottom of his bed in his room, and she now knew that he slept naked, that he loved to read a little before going to sleep.

She was stocking all of these little details, like valuable information, all these things that he did not say on his blog. On Friday night, Apollonia felt the pressure. She was worried that he would send her away the next day; tell her that, finally, one week was enough, and he did not want her to stay longer. She had not left since she had arrived there and she felt completely helpless to the idea of having to leave again, as if she doubted to find her way through the city, which seemed so far away now. She didn't want to leave, to go back to her old life, her boring job. She had forgotten all this with such ease that it was disconcerting. No lack, no frustration. No desire to leave.

On Saturday, she woke up nervously. She turned off the alarm clock near her that was there to remind her of her first daily task. She slipped under his duvet, got on all fours between his legs as he stretched slowly. She slowly licked on his balls, sucking them sometimes, or just passing her tongue everywhere. She was not to suck his cock, but rather just help him wake up. She loved it, deeply. She loved his warmth, the sweetness of his skin, his body still asleep, she loved his scent, his taste. She continued to please him with her tongue and her lips; she was enjoying these first minutes of her day as a gluttony, a generous favor he granted to her. He ended up interrupting her with a simple, "Thank you, Slave." So she got out of bed immediately, less awkwardly; she had learned to control her actions, not to rush, but to move with a little more elegance.

Perhaps one day she would have as much grace as Diane. She was kneeling, waiting for him to get up, and then she was kissing each of his feet and then the palm of his hand. He undid the lock of the chain in the greeting and she immediately went to prepare his coffee, unless he ordered anything else.

She had performed that four mornings in a row, but that day it was not the same. It may have been the last time. She poured his coffee and served a glass of orange juice that she have squeezed herself. She added some crackers and carried the tray to the table before going to kneel at her square. Every morning had been different; sometimes he did not know completely, or he demanded that she suck him at the same time he was taking his coffee. Sometimes again, he made her start cleaning immediately.

This Saturday morning, he began to ignore her at length. She was trembling, anxious. In her heart, she thought she had been up to the task. Of course, she had been punished many times. She had received the whip without flinching, and had never repeated the same fault twice. The wait did not end. He made her wait voluntarily. And he would not give in. The trial week ended at nine o'clock, at which time she had appeared at his door seven days earlier. He would wait for this precise time to talk to her.

He made her come and imposed her slave position, consisting of prostrating, breasts and face on the ground, arms outstretched; her back to him, she presented him with her rump. He made her wait a few minutes alone, and then came back behind her with a plug. He began by caressing her anus, and fingered her. She dilated slowly, sometimes spitting between her buttocks to make it easier. She offered herself without resistance. He then began to penetrate with the plug; he had to force a little, gently moving it in to open her body gradually. The base of the plug was wide and Apollonia had trouble not to manifest the pain he provoked by penetrating her fully.

Master Vincent stroked her pussy and clit a little, just enough to make her moan, and then he ordered her to her knees, facing him. He put his ball gag on her. He watched her. She wore only a pair of stockings, and her shoes with heels. It was his main outfit, the way he wanted it. Far from slaves with bare feet and irons, he preferred his stilettos and brand lingerie.

"There is something you did not do when you did the house chores. I want you to correct this mistake."

Apollonia, made dumb, looked up at him, and looked at him with incomprehension.

"The windows."

She understood. She had already thought about them, of course. But the windows were big and high, she would have shown herself completely for them to be clean.

"Open them, use a stool, and expose yourself in a most indecent manner, very important. You'll just put on your apron. Do not change. Commence immediately. And apply yourself. If you don't, the punishment will be terrible."

Before letting her do the job, he asked her to put pliers on her nipples. Nothing painful, just pretty little ones, like jewels, that dangled a few centimeters and that ended with small bells that tinkled at each movement. She felt right away terribly exposed and exhibited. She sometimes saw silhouettes through windows of the building opposite. There was even a man who smoked on his balcony, a floor lower, who did not fail to observe her, and to make his cigarette last. She was not sure he could see her completely, but her upper body, her naked breasts, her black gag in her mouth, he could not fail to see them. The first window was very difficult, mentally.

Apollonia was trying to hide herself, but it was impossible. Even without a stool, the glass began from the height of her knee to finish well above her head. Once she was away from the curtains, nothing hid her, especially when she was standing on the stool, windows wide open. As for the rest, she became accustomed and resigned herself. Very certainly, her Master's neighbors would see her, displaying her condition, humiliated by this morning exhibition. So what? Easy to say.

Apollonia did attempt to show no discomfort, no embarrassment, but her Master had seen her try as much as she could to hide herself. He had then seen the moment when she gave in, understanding that it was impossible to hide. He particularly liked that moment, when he felt that the spirit of one of his submissives had given up fighting, and surrendered herself to his orders, whatever they were. When this internal struggle, this conflict of morality and modesty that tormented her ended with no room left for a sincere carelessness. That was where he was reading most clearly the incipient abnegation of a submissive, her will to indulge, against all odds.

Apollonia always gave way quickly. She often had that fluttering second of resisting, but immediately it disappeared, sometimes with a flagrant difficulty, but very quickly, her soul was offered, her spirit entirely turned toward this condition that she had chosen. Her body no longer resisted. She belonged to him then fully. When the work was done, she put away her equipment and went to shower; she returned, kneeling at his feet, feverish.

"You have not been sloppy; it's good, Slave. My neighbors had to enjoy."

Apollonia had a nervous smile, but she could not help herself to feel happy that he was satisfied with her work.

"It is nine o'clock."

"Yes, Master, I know ..."

"Do you have anything to say to me, Slave?"

"Yes, Master ... I know we're at the end of my trial week. I wanted to tell you that on my side, I have loved every second, and that my desire to belong to you has never been so strong. I hope you'll keep me, and if that's the case, I swear to you a total obedience, and to give my body and soul to satisfy you and serve you properly."

Master Vincent had to guess half of her words as her voice had been a murmur. She lacked confidence and ease. Despite this, if he had any doubts, her words had finished convincing him. How could he refuse such a gift?

"I know I told you that I will not spare you during this week. However, I was pretty soft with you. Not by desire to preserve you, but because I was not very present, and that the opportunity to test you did not come up. Know that it will not always be so. If I keep you, you'll go through really hard times."

Apollonia smiled, without him being able to see her, because she had lowered her head. She guessed at his words that he had made his decision, and that she was in his favor. And in the end, she did not feel worried as to its future difficulties. Even if he had emphasized it, she felt confident and thought that on the whole, the days ahead would look like those she had already lived, neither more nor less. And that suited her perfectly. To tell the truth, she was hoping for a little more spice sometimes. It was a test on the moment, but afterwards, she was happy to have overcome it.

"You've been almost irreproachable since you've been here. You surprised me, I did not think you'd adapt so quickly and that you would like to live as such. So you deserve to stay. I am keeping you for four weeks. In four Saturdays, at this hour, we will have this same conversation. You will stay, or you will depart."

"Yes, Master. Thank you for keeping me ..."

Master Vincent approached her so that she made contact with him. Cheek against his thigh, she dared to clasp his legs between her arms and hug him against her knees, her Lord and Master. He stroked her hair and they remained like that for a long time. He finally pulled back and put a kiss on her forehead, as he did to reward her or to show her a little tenderness.

She was happy, fully.

PART THREE

Apollonia felt fulfilled. Precious. This feeling of well-being completely encompassed her like a warm blanket. She savored all these emotions. She considered it a real victory that he wanted to keep her. That meant she had some skills, she had been able to satisfy someone as demanding as her Master. She felt more confident. More beautiful even.

Master Vincent tied her down the hall, near the bathroom, with just enough chain length for her to go to the toilet. He left her a bowl of water and something to eat in a plate that he put on the floor. She handed him his coat, a little sad, because she understood that he would leave for a long time. She kissed his feet to wish him a good day as she had to do when she woke up, at bedtime, when he went away, and when he came back. A humble slave kiss that she adored.

She remained alone. Everything was silent. Empty. Where was he going? Was he having lunch with Diane? It was the weekend; Apollonia was expecting to see him appear in the evening or the next day. Without doubt she was still going to have to attend their meetings. She did not know if she would have preferred not to witness them and stay alone, or if she preferred to be present even with no participation. For the first time since she was there she thought she would have liked to browse Master Vincent's blog, to see if he had written new texts. To know if he spoke of her.

She had often observed him when he was on his computer, trying to guess that, but he could be doing many other things.

Apollonia felt alone. Still, she was happy to be accepted for a month. And then to these questions, to this loneliness, was added his lack of desire for sex. She had not taken it the day before, she just enjoyed his mouth. She wanted him, at every second. To guess that she was going to see him with Diane, no doubt the same evening, and so he would not touch her, made her realize how much she wanted him.

In anticipation of her frustration to come, she lay down on the floor. He did not allow her a cushion in the day, so there was not the benefit of too much comfort. She moved slowly and caressed; it was the first time she did so, alone, without his order.

She hesitated a moment, doubtful of having the right, but, after all, he did not forbid her. She was already soaked. She closed her eyes and imagined him in front of her. She remembered all those moments when he had observed her, in shameless positions in which he forced her to expose herself. When he told her that she should be ashamed to behave like that, like a little bitch in heat, at the same time he lashed the inside of her thighs, so that they spread more to the floor.

She remembered those times when he forced her to repeat that she was a little slut, and ask him for his cock, lying down as she was on the floor, indecent, but boiling with cravings.

She remembered his smile that she sometimes saw when he felt she was at the edge of her enjoyment, and he decided to leave her thus, without even a touch. She enjoyed—too fast for her taste, she would have liked to enjoy still more of this pleasure—those images which paraded before her eyes. She did not know how to control herself. She would do a little more later, no doubt. The day had not ended.

†

When she finally guessed they were in the corridor, she hurried to kneel. He arrived as she had foreseen, with Diane. She prepared their dinner. Master Vincent decided to use her as a coffee table, and put his hat and Diane's on her back. It was not so much this position that she felt was humiliating, it was the fact that they both ignored her completely.

No gesture, no caress, no word. She was furniture, neither more nor less. She felt relegated to the rank of an object, and unable to explain why it excited her, why she liked being treated that way, and why, despite everything, it remained difficult. Her shoulders were stiff and she found it very hard to keep the perfect position. After the meal, he made her stand up, legs apart, and gave her two big candles that she had to hold. One in each hand. She had to keep her arms away from her body and keep the candles in front of her, like a living candlestick.

He put a gag-ring on her which, unlike the ball gag, left her mouth open and drove her to drool more. He stared at her for a moment before putting a blindfold over her eyes. She stayed like that. An eternity. She did not see anything that was happening, but as in the previous week, she heard their words, their cries, and their moans. She felt like he was doing everything possible to make Diane moan again and again until it became unbearable. She wanted him. She wanted him as ever.

He saw in her posture that she was exhausted, and after having repeated this position several times, he finally removed the candles, already diminished in her hands, and ordered her to take her slave position. Apollonia knelt before him, putting her cheek to the ground, thighs well apart. At his order she put her hands on her buttocks to move them further apart.

She stayed like that, arched, offered to a penetration that would come. She understood that he pushed one of the candles in her ass and it made her emit an uncontrolled moan. The candle in place, there was no back and forth likely to give her pleasure, nothing, she just felt a little fulfilled, but instead of a pleasant sensation, it frustrated her more. She was still blinded and her mouth constrained by the ring; she felt her saliva run under her cheek, unable to avoid it. The wax began to spread on her skin, and it was much more sensitive than when hands ran on her.

She liked this sensation. She heard their cries, she guessed their gestures. She knew he was taking her by the hips, violently, sinking fully in. She could hear them panting, she could imagine breathless from so much sex. Diane was abandoning herself and screaming her pleasure without restraint. And then she heard him enjoy, in a deep rattle. She heard her breath, right after, her breathing, gently disturbed by the enjoyment, which slowly resumed its normal rhythm. Apollonia was an object.

She had never felt it so much. It was a sensation of the most contradictory. She loved, and she did not like, all at once. She liked not to love, maybe? Unless, on the contrary, she was ashamed to love. The candle was almost consumed, she felt that the wax was becoming hotter, but at the same time, an already thick layer had solidified on her perineum and her hips. She had pain in the neck, the position became infernal. Her shoulders also were really hurting, but for nothing in the world would she have budged.

Finally, she felt a breath on her buttocks, and guessed he had extinguished the flame. He removed the candle and ordered her to remove her headband and serve them a glass of wine. He forbade her to remove the wax stuck to her skin. This gave her a funny feeling of having this amalgam solidified between the buttocks, but the wax broke loose quite quickly following the change of position and movement.

She still had the ring, more terrible than the ball that held a little saliva, but there she could not do anything. Her saliva flowed in a long net from her mouth, along her chin, from her breasts to her navel and lower still. Strangely, she felt more humiliated by that than having held the role of candlestick during their session. She had already been forced to this gag and harshly punished when she tried to wipe her chin with the back of her hand; she was resigned. He wanted to belittle her before Diane; she had to submit to it.

But Diane did not even look at her. She was on her knees between the Master's legs, her head on his thigh, her look toward him, toward his naked torso. Apollonia went a little on the side, as a plateau. She kept her head down, which accentuated the amount of saliva flowing from her mouth. Master Vincent watched her for a long moment, with a smile. He was amused to see this, and aware of the efforts she made to please him. He got up and came back to her, ordering her to put out her tongue, since the ring allowed it, and put a clothespin on it with the order not to move, and especially not to knock the clip. It was a real constraint, impossible to think of anything else as she had to focus so much on this position.

She had terrible jaw pain, but fortunately, the forceps were not painful. She was not content to stay that way. She had her tongue outside her mouth and was having a lot of trouble swallowing; she was mentally trying. She could not take it anymore. She had a dry throat, she was in pain, she was thirsty, she felt that mentally she cracked slowly. For something as stupid as a ring, a constrained mouth. Master Vincent turned to her.

"Is it painful?"

She nodded.

"All the better. That's the point. I like to see you that way. And you're here to please me, are not you?"

She nodded again. She wanted to cry; she felt like a claustrophobic of the mouth.

"I forbid you to be weak, Slave. If I see you disrespecting the position I am ordering you, I will impose it still more, and you will be punished. It's understood? You go stay that way for a moment."

Apollonia lowered her head a little, defeated, submissive. She had unintentionally manifested his difficulty; this had been read on his face too blatantly. He did not like it. She managed to take it on, with a lot of trouble. She resigned herself to the fact that he loved to let go. She saw it: the features of his face, to his breath, to the relaxation of his shoulders. She remained still, holding the tray on which the glasses were both empty. Neither her Master nor Diana looked at her. Nobody cared anymore for her presence. She was alone in this constraint that she had finally imposed upon herself. She had wanted so much to live like this that it was impossible for her to feel pity, even internally.

Finally, he allowed her to go and rest, and this was a great relief. Once alone in the kitchen, she wanted to crumble in tears, but managed to hold on. Master Vincent ordered her to join them in the bathroom, and to stand at disposal, two bath towels placed on her forearms. She liked to wait like that usually when he was alone. This was different. Diane came first out of the shower and seized a bath towel, without any particular reaction to Apollonia. She acted as if it was natural that she be there. Natural, but above all, totally indifferent. She seemed really only an object in her eyes. An object without value.

Diane got dressed. Obviously, she was not going to spend the night in the apartment, and Apollonia could not help but smile, despite the pain that had not stopped. Master Vincent rescued her finally from the clip and its gag. That's when her tongue hurt her, almost refusing to take its place after these long minutes of stress. She finally took possession of her mouth. She had to stay in the entrance for a few moments, then Diana arrived, and Apollonia handed her her coat. She helped her to put it on while keeping her head down, humbly. She went to open the door when Master Vincent held it back.

"Hold on. I want you to fuck her feet."

Apollonia remained frozen. Three, four seconds. More than usual. More than he accepted. At the moment she really understood the order, and overcame this difficulty of acceptance that had caused the delay, she was preparing to kneel before Diane to execute herself. But Master Vincent interrupted her, and seized her by the hair.

"You have a problem with this order, Slave?!"

"No, Master, no ... forgive me ..."

"Why do you not obey immediately?"

"I beg your pardon, I did not expect it ... I am sorry ... I'll do it, Master."

"You can do it? But I count on it! Come here."

He dragged her into the living room, where there was more room, and threw her to the ground. Apollonia could not believe such a reaction, but she deeply regretted not having obeyed immediately; she would have avoided all that, and he would have been proud of her. Because of her hesitation, she was going to have a difficult time.

"Look at me!"

Apollonia was on her knees, her hands on the ground; she raised her head, and received a slap, violent, which surprised her. It was the first time he had slapped her. Apollonia felt particularly ashamed to have made a mistake that deserved that, and more than that, that all this passed in front of Diane. She swallowed her pride, but guessed that it would be very difficult for him to let go of.

"Who are you?!"

"Your slave, Master ..."

"What is your role here?"

"To obey you, Master."

Another slap hit her hard.

"Then why do you not do it?!"

"I'm sorry, Master ... I was going to do it ... I ..."

"That's enough! When I order, you obey! Immediately and without any delay!"

"Yes, Master, sorry ... I will obey ..."

"It would be in your interest that it does not happen again. Take your folded position."

"Yes, Master …"

Apollonia swallowed her tears, somehow. This scene, this position to take in front of Diane, after all that had already passed during the evening, seemed to her too much humiliation. But she complied, a ball in her stomach that she displeased him again. The tight throat of being lowered so much. She positioned herself standing, back to him, legs wide apart, and folded in two to put her hands on the ground.

He made her wait like that, enjoying all the power he had over her. He wanted her to be ashamed of herself. That she be deeply ashamed of her situation, of her position, but above all her fault and her status of bad slave. He wanted her to feel his disappointment, his anger. He wanted it to spread deep within her, for never again would she want to live such a moment. He spoke, his voice hard, his tone dry and sharp.

"Do you think I'm proud of you when I give you an order and you are so late in obeying me? Do you realize that? Do you want me to be someone who is incapable of being respected by his slave?"

"No, Master, sorry, I beg you, forgive me ... it will never happen again ... I promise you ..."

That was where he was coming from. Create in this conviction that any refusal of obedience would have consequences much more serious than any act he might impose on her.

"I admit that tonight, I doubt it! Imagine if it was spent

in a club, or at a friend's house? And you have this attitude? Do you want to shame me?"

"No, Master, really, no ... I ..."

"Silence! I have all the rights over you. It's you who came to offer yourself to me, and who swore obedience to me. So, obey, whatever I order you, at once."

"Yes, Master."

Her voice was whispering, she was sobbing at the same time, deeply ashamed of her fault. She did not allow herself to find it unfair. He was right, she had promised him obedience—she had not kept her word. His anger was justified. Yet she would have done it, she knew it, she had just been slow to obey. It was not because she had disobeyed. Master Vincent was not unfair, but he was tough. Very hard even.

"I warned you that you would never have the same rights as Diane. That you would always be inferior to her. You should obey her if I decide. You remember it?"

"Yes, Master."

"Your attitude should be as irreproachable with her as it is with me. It's understood?"

"Yes, Master."

Apollonia heard him talking to Diane who seemed rather amused by the situation. He asked her if she wanted to punish her, since her fault concerned her. Diane pretended to hesitate, as if she was not sure how to do it. Then she gave her the first shot of the whip.

"Is it strong enough, Master?"

"No, not enough."

Diane snapped the leather much harder on Apollonia's buttocks; she was still in a bent position, offered to her blows.

"It's good like this. No weaker. Thirty strokes."

"Yes, Master."

Diane applied, giving fifteen shots on each buttock. She was hitting hard, and seemed to like this little punishment.

"I really like to see you whip her ass."

"I will do it every time you ask me, Master."

"I know."

He paused for a few seconds, watching the buttocks streaked with Apollonia's blood; he saw his body move to the rhythm of her sobs.

"Here, Slave, on your knees."

She rushed to his feet.

"Kneel in front of Diane, and ask her forgiveness for your attitude unworthy of your condition in her presence."

She complied and said her words of excuse with a knotted throat. She had a pain in her stomach as she felt bad and shameful to lower herself thus before her.

"It's good. Now, obey."

Apollonia leaned her elbows on the floor, and kissed each of Diane's shoes. Her throat was tight.

"It was not complicated! Yes?"

"No, Master ..."

"From now on, you will do it as with me. Before taking her coat, when she arrives, and after giving it to her, when she leaves. Even if I am not present. You have heard? I do not want to have to say it again."

"Yes, Master. I understand. I will obey."

He knew she had yielded, deep inside herself. She had not only agreed to do so, she understood that she had to do it because he ordered it. It was his role. He would be attentive to its speed of execution the next time, and then it would become a ritual among the others, neither more nor less. But he knew that would condition her mind to obedience.

She was going to lose all reluctance, even involuntarily, to obey. Executing an order quickly would become a reflex primarily, even before she realized what he was imposing on her. Apollonia remained motionless, barely up. She left Diane to kneel before him, to wish him a sweet night, and to leave at last. He grabbed Apollonia by the hair and made her follow him, on all fours. He led her to the couch, where he sat down.

"Do you find me too hard with you?"

"No, Master."

He stroked her cheek, pulling her a little closer to him; she kept her cheek against his knee, and she almost blamed herself for loving this contact so much.

"The trial period is over. You had time to take your marks for everyday life. You know what you have to do day to day. But your presence here is not limited to that."

"I know, Master."

"I did not like your reluctance just now. Truly not."

Apollonia lowered her head a little, distraught to see him back again on this hesitation for which she had already been punished.

"I understand, Master."

"Tonight, I wanted to keep you in my room, but I decided that from now on, every day you commit a fault, even minimal, you will not be entitled to. There is no reason that I should reward you so, if you behave badly."

"Yes, Master ..."

"Go shower and place your cushion in the entrance. So you do not forget that it is a night of punishment, you will sleep with your hands tied around your back. It will be very uncomfortable, I guess. If it keeps you awake, you'll take the time to meditate on your actions."

The night was indeed very painful for Apollonia. She had to harden, and above all, no longer make mistakes. This punishment had no other purpose than to send it to this conclusion. He educated her, and one by one he broke her reluctance. She was aware of it. She knew he wanted her to not make a mistake again.

He set it up, as one trains a domestic animal to serve and

be useful. A reward when acted well, a punishment when acted badly. It was nothing but dressage. She knew it and she accepted it.

†

He stayed there most of the next day. He made her do a more thorough cleaning than usual, and to do the windows that had not been done the day before. Master Vincent had felt that the previous evening had been difficult, a little too much maybe. He knew that it was necessary to cultivate a delicate balance so that kind of relationship can continue. It was not about giving in, or showing compassion, but about education. He could not just punish her when she was hurting something, even if, in theory, a slave did not have to be pampered.

He had watched her all morning, coming and going with her maid's apron and her gag-ball, and had found her particularly exciting. So he did not really have to force himself to call her, and order her to suck him. She applied herself more than before. She saw the end of her punishment, as if it were a sign that he wanted her again and that she was truly forgiven. He made her stand up and he caressed her for a long time, forcing her to keep her hands on her head, and move on his fingers. She was boiling at the slightest contact with him. If at first he wanted to keep her moaning, she gave way very quickly.

He had magician's fingers, and knew exactly what to do to make her bend with pleasure. She was already panting when he made her sit on him, back against his torso. The position was not very simple because it was resting on his thighs, but it was the first time he took it so. She loved all those first times as a slave, finally, as long as it did not concern a fault! She went up and down on his cock, she impaled hard, penetrated deeply by contracting her muscles internally, then opened gently so that it felt like a caress from deep within herself.

She managed the rhythm of her movements, according to his own, forgetting the muscles in her thighs that needed a break. Master Vincent played with her buttocks, he seemed to enjoy his efforts, and she loved to take it so. Then, after long minutes in tune, he straightened up, sticking his body to her, clasping her almost tenderly with his arms. She did not dare move, she enjoyed being so close to him, the way he hugged her, the warmth of his body. She could have cried for the pleasure that only existed in this world. Another pleasure, that little can understand. He pulled her gently, taking his time with her.

He faced her, spreading her thighs, and took her on his bed, for the first time. She gasped and enjoyed without restraint.

He was playing with her clit and also her breasts, his fingers that went from her belly to her breasts, then dived into her mouth. Then he returned her, unceremoniously, as if to erase those moments too voluptuous to a slave, slamming her ass and spreading her buttocks to take her doggy style. He took her in all positions, anyway, catching her firmly by the hips, playing with her tits and her clit while moving in intensely. She was losing her footing, she was sweating, she was out of breath, she screamed like she had never screamed before, lost in an abandonment of pleasure and intense submission.

He let go sometimes, pushing her away, ordering her to crawl between his thighs and suck his cock full of cum. She had to always place herself so that he could stroke her, or penetrate her with his fingers, entertaining her orifices while she was busy with her tongue, her mouth. He loved when she felt pleasure at the same time she sucked him. She let go so much she became more enterprising, more perverse. She was losing modesty, all restraint.

She dared to separate her legs more, both because she knew it was what he wanted, and because she wanted to. Because that excited her to offer herself and feel immodest. She sucked him too with more ardor, daring to play with her tongue, stretching it out as much as a hungry bitch, before taking it deep into her mouth, aspiring, and titillating his glans with the tip of her tongue.

He ended up coming on her, to take pleasure. He wanted to see her getting lost in this, see her screaming her pleasure, cheeks red. He wanted to see her enjoy it one last time, at the same time as him. He honored her, in a groan, his skin glistening with sweat, out of breath. Then he lay down, savoring the moment just after.

She remained a moment to regain her senses, without knowing what to do, hesitating to leave the bed. But he grabbed her by the arm, and then made her lie down against him. She did not dare move, nor even breathe, not to interrupt this delicious moment. She had her cheek against his chest and quietly smelled the scent of his skin; she let herself be rocked by the beating of his heart which slowly resumed its natural rhythm.

He kept her close for a moment; she loved every second, it was beyond what she could have imagined, realizing how strong her feelings were. Too strong, without doubt. She had begun to love him even before she met him, just by reading his words and imagining him. How could she have remained impassive while living by his side, under his roof, being permanently at his disposal? Sometimes she realized that it would have been easier not to like him, so without doubt she would not have wanted this slave life and would have ended all this madness after just having a little taste.

But what she felt was more than feelings in love, it was more than that. It was the powerful link that was being built. She did not like him as one loves a man, but as one venerates a divinity. All this would have seemed completely incomprehensible to the rest of the world. But in their world, there was this link, uniting servile beings with half-gods, submissives and slaves to lords, masters. She had read this so many times, and this time she touched its reality.

The evening was more difficult for Apollonia. She understood that he was preparing to join Diane and she would spend the night with him in the apartment. She ate alone and fell asleep. When they arrived, he woke her up and she had to resign herself to the new ritual, and fuck Diane's feet at the same time as those of her Master. She served them a drink, and then he sent her away. Apollonia had trouble going back to sleep, always overwhelmed by conflicting feelings that obsessed her. And she was mentally trying.

By her reasoning, it was only her second weekend, and she was going to get used. Soon all that would be normal. She was a slave, and he treated her as he wanted. And that was what she had come for. His side woman was still too present, and this part brought to the surface all those emotions that made her fragile. This restraint to obey, the day before, was nothing but a hint of pride, it was the woman who did not want to feel belittled in front of Diane.

And again, it was a little jealousy that was turning and turning her without sleep, knowing they were both completely indifferent to her presence. Yet she did not want to annihilate everything that made her a woman, she did not want to become a soulless being, a simple machine of flesh ready to obey.

She wanted to be more than a body constrained. She

wanted to keep feeling. She loved to feel sometimes a tear of emotion running down her cheek, just because he was kissing her shoulder after having taken her. She loved to feel her mind fighting against herself and ending up submitting. Hardening was not incompatible with feeling. And if she were to have more difficult moments, she had to accept it as a form of counterpart to those sensations she cherished so much.

†

She was gradually becoming a perfect domestic slave. She had understood everything she had to do. He had only very rarely needed to correct her. Yet he was still extremely demanding and he did not let anything pass. He inspected from time to time her cleaning, and when he wanted to, he always had something to complain about, if only for the pleasure of punishing her, and to make sure that she would not ever let go her vigilance to do her best. He was brimming with imagination to always remind her of her condition. In this case, she did not feel like a housekeeper. He imposed on her to always wear a gag, whether with the ball or the ring, sometimes on her breasts the ones with the bells, or others; they were sonorous but painful to wear in movement.

He also liked to force her to wear the plug during household tasks. As he had taught her the art of getting ready intimately, he could take advantage of the fact that her ass was well dilated to take her thus, when she had finished her work. He liked to whisper in her ear that she was "his ass-fucked little maid" and she had learned to love that. He had also put tongs in her intimate lips, ballasted a small weight so that it was very unpleasant and a little painful after a moment. Often, he accumulated several accessories at the same time. He liked to see her wander in the apartment— so constrained, but seemingly unperturbed in her work. He sometimes came next to her to observe her closely, which completely deconcentrated her.

He would watch her behind his shoulder and give her whips of a whip or a long martinet, just to disrupt her. Sometimes he caressed her, imposing not to interrupt, while she was washing the dishes or working in the kitchen, or cleaning the bathtub, leaning forward. It was never for her to just clean up as a housewife, she was a slave to his service, and bore all his abuse. And thanks to that, it was never the same. Once, for fun, he ordered her to perform a task with a small vibrator stuck in her pussy, that he could operate from a distance. Once activated, this one did not hold in place, and slipped as soon as she moved; even if she worked the muscles of her vagina as much as possible to keep it in her, it was impossible, so she had to constantly hold it, with one hand. The constant vibrations gave her pleasure in spite of herself, and she could not manage at all to focus.

He loved seeing her so distraught, doing everything much less quickly because she could only work with one hand. He paused in his own occupations to observe her with a smirk, vacuuming, hand between legs to hold the vibrator, her mind troubled, her cheeks red, and at the edge of enjoyment. When she was done, he forced her to keep the vibrator in, even in the shower, and come back with it always between her legs. She had to take her offering position, shamelessly dismissed, hands behind the knees to keep her legs well open.

He had observed for some moments the sex-toy vibrating, impaled, before playing with it and rolling it over her clit. Apollonia was so excited that she could not do it anymore, and was dying. She felt burning and could not restrain herself from enjoying, almost immediately. She had a gaping, inflated pussy, excited, liquid of desire. He had wanted her, to take her thus, immediately, but her position was too beautiful and she seemed perfectly willing to taste something else, that she had not told him. He penetrated her gently with his fingers, then he began to exercise a pressure while holding the tip of the vibrator on her clit with the other hand.

He sank into her more and more. It was getting a bit painful, but that feeling of being taken, to be forced by his hand, excited her. She was in such a state that anything could have given her pleasure. She offered herself and felt his hand wider in her. It hurt her, more and more. He forced, and the pressure in her was accentuated, until she felt her body letting go slowly, and the pain subside. She was fisted. She loved that feeling to be completely fulfilled, to be taken well, physically. He kept his hand still in her and played more with the vibrator to make her cum.

He then felt it suddenly contract with pleasure on his hand. He retreated slowly, very softly, and that brought her further delicious sensations, without pain this time. He took advantage of her a long time after that, using from her mouth and her whole body, still burning with excitement. Another time, he had been harder with her, and he had imposed to do all her household kneeling, legs held by a spreader bar. It had been a very physical test which had left bruises on her knees for several days. His imagination seemed boundless to coerce and possess her. Thus, the household was never just a domestic chore—that, but real and intense moments of submission. She loved especially those everyday moments, because he was always present, and it was quite rare that he ignored her from one end to the other part of her task.

Sometimes, at the weekend, she had to fulfill this chore in the presence of Diane, and that was something else. She felt much more humiliated; even if by force, she knew perfectly what she had to do. She felt her eyes when she was busy in the living room, and she was struggling to get used to it. Master Vincent, who had never hidden his pleasure from humiliating her in front of his submissive, spared her nothing when he was so. He knew that everything was more restrictive and difficult for Apollonia when Diane was present. So he imposed more constraints still. He made her rush herself even in slave position when her rump faced them as they quietly drank their coffee. Before, she had to get a little bit of lubricant and he penetrated with his fingers until it allowed him to introduce the plug, which was never easy or fast. Especially in this position. He would then put the tongs with bells on her intimate lips, and the claws that hurt on the nipples.

After a few whips, and a last humiliating word, Apollonia could get to work, imagining Diana's smile, half mocking, half admiring of her abnegation. Apollonia got used to it somehow. She knew he liked to belittle her even more in the presence of Diana, he had told her so. He really liked it. It made him hard. It was always Diane who took advantage of this excitement, but it was Apollonia who did it originally, and she clung to that. She was there for his pleasure, it did not matter how she gave it to him. He liked to treat her so, and in a way, she liked him to do it. And she preferred that to ignorance. Nothing was worse than when he was with Diane, and she was relegated to the entrance, without even being able to see or hear them.

Sometimes he called her and she rushed to her knees at his feet, to serve him, but he did not want anything other than a coffee or a glass of wine. He did not even look at her. She came back with a tray and remained transparent. When they had finished, he did not even take the time to tell her to return to her place, he just made a gesture, almost contemptuous, toward the door, to tell her that she had to go away, and she ran, head lowered. She had come to see another form of humiliation.

More perverse finally, more cerebral. It was easy for him to impose an indecent position and hit her in front of Diane. Tell her raw, vulgar words and have fun repeating them, to make sure she did not forget her condition. The desired effect was immediate and undoubtedly funny, for Diane and for him. Ignorance was something else; it was more subtle, harder. It was a humiliation that remained deeply rooted in her and troubled her more than having to be penetrated by a large plug in an open ass, facing Diane.

Sometimes when they arrived, or left late at night, and Apollonia slept, he liked to wake her, just to see her fuck his feet. He did not even speak to her, and she not to him. Her ritual accomplished, she remained a little while on her knees, time to realize that they were already gone, without even a look or a word. What she felt was a profound complexity. But no doubt she felt like a slave.

Gradually, he imposed more and more things on her for Diane. He ordered her to wait for her when she was under the shower, systematically. Even if he was not there. She had to give her the towel when she came out. He told her that if Diane asked her to wipe her, she had to obey. And she had to do it just like with him, suck the drops with her mouth, then gently dab her body, everywhere, from top to bottom, and at the end, kneeling, stretch out the towel, so that she could finish if necessary. So she had to bow down, wait for an order or to be told she was no longer needed. Apollonia was troubled by Diane's omnipresence, though fortunately it was very rare that she was there during the week. But weekends were always tiring because of her. Apollonia had come to offer herself to her Master, not to a submissive.

He had warned her from the start, and she had nothing to complain about, but she feared it would get bigger. Master Vincent often asked Diana to punish her with the whip. Sometimes he even reported the punishments of the week, so that they were applied by her when she came. He liked that. The days passed thus, never the same, despite the rehearsals. Master Vincent was sometimes very hard, and sometimes also he showed her so much tenderness and attention that she almost thought she did not deserve as much. She loved it the most when he took her against him after having enjoyed it. He would talk to her a little bit about things. She drank in his words, her eyes sparkling. He sometimes asked her if she loved the slave life, but she did not really like to let him do it. She wanted to forget that it was a choice. What always had been the choice. Forgetting that she had only one word to say to go. It was precisely in those moments that she was fully aware that she was not a slave the way she would have liked it.

Without even the choice to end it, and especially, without a deadline. She felt like a rented slave. In the interim. She was already dreading the day she should leave, at worse in a few days, at best in a year. How could she return to a normal life? Do as if nothing had happened and resume her life where she left off? She was avoiding thinking about it as much as possible; wondering about it terrified her.

†

The weekend before the last week of the test was very disturbing. Master Vincent called her when he took his coffee on Friday. He gazed at her for a long time, and made her look at him, raising her chin. He seemed a little upset, tense.

"Do you sincerely feel able to endure everything to be mine?"

"Yes, Master …"

She said yes, but her voice trembled.

"No cleaning today; go shower. And hurry up."

Apollonia complied, a ball in her stomach. She was both ready to be tested, and at the same time terrified of not being up to it. When he was ready, he ordered her to take her toiletries and her makeup, and put on her coat. It was her first time out of the house.

After being shut at home all this time, she had ceased to believe that she would ever leave. Excitation exceeded this fear. He covered her eyes and guided her to his car. She felt disturbed to appear in the middle of the street with a blindfold, but submitted fully to him. He waited a few moments, then ordered her to open her coat and keep her legs well apart. She was not simply transient, she remained his slave, and no doubt he was amused to see her in this position at his side. They drove for a long time, silently. She was biting her tongue not to ask him where he was taking her. In any case, she had to surrender to him, wherever he decided to take her.

They ended up arriving in a place still unknown to her. He told her it was a mansion lost in the heart of beautiful neighborhoods, with a large porch, a square courtyard, and paved parking. But she could not see anything. The car stopped. He opened the door and guided her. She felt the cobblestones slide under her high heels. She followed him slowly, a little feverish.

He had tied a leash to the ring of her necklace. He held her with one hand by the arm, and with the other by that leash. Apollonia was worried; she thought he was going to lend her to someone. She sensed a heavy door opening, and heard a female voice greet her Master with respect. He did not answer, or maybe just nodded his head. Apollonia felt him take off his coat, and he ordered her to do the same. She was naked underneath, except for her stockings and a garter belt, but she obeyed immediately, guessing the place conducive to this kind of obedience. She was rid of it and she smiled at the idea that another slave, without doubt also undressed, held the same role she endorsed habitually.

The voice invited them to follow her and Master Vincent pulled Apollonia by her leash, holding her closer to her collar to better guide her, but he had let go of her arm. Walking in the dark was more difficult. It was not a question of lack of confidence, but rather an innate reflex that pushed her to caution. She wanted to put her hands a little forward, to feel more reassured, but obviously he did not like this gesture, and ordered her to put her hands at the back, and to give them back to him. They advanced like this. A corridor, a door that opened and then closed, parquet, carpet, stairs descending. This time he held her so that she would not fall. Something deep inside her made her understand that she had to appreciate these moments against his body, because a difficulty still never contemplated was waiting for her at the bottom of these steps.

"He will join you in a few moments. May I serve you, one way or another, sir?"

"I'll be fine, no."

Apollonia had been appreciative of the tone and words spoken by the submissive who had welcomed them; she felt her abnegation and the quality of her training. She guessed that she had practiced to pronounce these words, ready to afford to entertain the guest of her Master when he arrived. Apollonia felt still clumsy and novice in comparison. No doubt the confrontation with other people was going to be difficult and maybe painful, but most certainly it would be beneficial to her apprenticeship.

There were footsteps and a door that opened. Some exchanges and cordial politeness between the man and Master Vincent, and then a metallic noise of chains.

"Is it okay for you?"

"Yes, it is perfect. That's exactly what I wanted."

Then he spoke to her, ordering her to take off her shoes, and her lingerie. Apollonia complied, still blind. The submissive gently took her things, assuring her to take good care of them. Her Master led her a few steps forward and removed her headband. Her eyes blinked a little after this period from darkness but she quickly understood the purpose of the visit.

A cage.

She was in the middle, in a big cage, or rather a small cell. About five or six square meters, a place only seen in movies. There was a toilet and a sink, no shower. No seat or bed, just one cover on the concrete floor. Two of the walls were in cut stone, the other two sides in prison bars. Around this, there was a kind of large, ancient, vaulted cellar with arcades, exposed stones, and beams. There was nothing, no accessories or anything that suggested a kind of private dungeon, just this cell that had seen many others, no doubt. She looked at her Master with so much trepidation that she knew her attitude would cause him problems. Her body betrayed her; she trembled.

"I have to leave for a few days. This place is like a kennel for little bitches of your kind. You will be fine here in the meantime. You will be wise."

"How long, Master?"

The slap was sharp, but Apollonia was not even surprised, realizing her fault at the same time as she did it. It was both the question, but also the tone.

"As long as I want, Slave!"

"Yes, Master, sorry."

"You know I can add constraints to your captivity? This place is like a good restaurant, I order 'to the card' which will be imposed on you. And I can attend where I am from, thanks to the little camera placed there, which films you permanently. Do you want me to order some torture? I did not foresee it, but if your attitude is not correct, I will not hesitate to do it."

"Forgive me, Master."

He spoke to the man who was standing a little behind.

"You'll add thirty swift strokes, morning, noon, and evening, at the same time as the meals."

"It will be done."

Apollonia felt faint, slowly becoming aware of the reality of what was happening.

"Do you have something to say, Slave? Or do you want I allow you to be delivered to whoever wants you? His friend list is impressive and I'm sure you would have a lot of success."

Apollonia shook her head, not daring to look up at him, fear of doing or saying anything that might be worth such a treatment.

"You have nothing to fear here. I will watch you. I'll be back soon. Do not disappoint me."

"Yes, Master …"

He laid a hard kiss on her forehead and walked out of the cell. The man then closed the gate with a chain and a padlock. Then they both left. The submissive was gone meanwhile; Apollonia had not seen her again. She remained alone. Naked. Unable to move, in a kind of state of shock. After a few minutes, she realized that her attitude would change nothing, that she had to submit, and to wait, since such was the desire of her Master. In time he would come back to look for her, and her life at his feet would resume. She rolled into a ball in the blanket, and waited.

It was obvious that Master Vincent could not take her on a trip or weekend if he was going to see family, or just because he did not want to. As he refused to let her free from his movements at home when he was not there, this solution was ideal for him. If Apollonia had known that such places existed, no doubt she would have been less surprised. She was slowly becoming used to the idea. Except for the martinet, nothing else would happen to her.

She was captive. For real. It was the first time she had felt this by this point. No one except her Master knew where she was. She had no way to reach anyone. She was actually a prisoner of a cell, in a place she did not know anything of. Nor did she know her jailers. The only thing that allowed her to not panic was the little red light on the webcam that faced her cage, which connected her to her Master. At least she hoped. Would he really take the time to look at her, while leaving for the weekend? Had he gone with Diane? Leaving her here, in a cage?

Apollonia had a very difficult time. She felt like a really bitchy animal of which one is glad to get rid of for the holidays, to no more have the constraint of taking care of it.

She sobbed for a long time before falling into a half-restless sleep. She had no idea of the time or the time that was passing; he had gone so fast, almost without saying goodbye, the spirit already occupied by what he had planned afterwards. Dropping her there had been a formality before his departure, a material constraint to manage. She thought he was taking her somewhere to make her live out her condition on the outside, to change her everyday life, but it was not so. He just needed to get rid of her some days. She resented him. And ... she was mad at him. She did not know where she was.

Someone came at last, no doubt the young woman who had opened the door. She must not be yet twenty, and she was beautiful like an angel. She was barefoot and wearing a white dress; completely transparent, it was more a sail. Two wide steel bracelets at the ankles and one around her neck clearly showed her condition. She wore a heavy plateau humbly. A man accompanied her. He was tall, with a shaved head, and rather scary.

He was dressed in black and held a long swift in his hand. Apollonia shuddered as she thought about what was waiting for her, but did not want to disappoint her Master. She knelt where she was, lowered her head and waited for him to tell her what to do. She did not have to wait long. The man opened the gate and entered. He ordered her to come back and get on all fours. Hardly was she in place than the martinet slammed violently on her buttocks. It was much more painful than what Master Vincent imposed on her.

He was hitting without state of mind, mechanically, as if he were acquainted with the job before he could go home.

The thirty shots given, he went away, closing the gate behind him. Without a word. The woman had laid the tray on the ground in the meantime and had already withdrawn. Apollonia stayed in shock for a moment before wiping her tears and curled up again in the blanket. Master Vincent had ordered three sets of thirty rounds a day. It was a lot.

It was too much. And then she remembered why she was subjected to this difficult treatment. Because she had asked him how long she would stay there indecently, in front of someone, more so. If she had not said anything, she would have just been imprisoned, but not beaten. She was angry. From him, for being so cruel. From herself, for not to being able to obey the orders swiftly. She ended up eating, it was lunch. The wait was going to seem endless. She took a long time to accept this situation. Understand and accept the will of her Lord and Master, and resign herself. She did not give up until late in the night, after a second meal and a second series of swings.

What was happening to her was only an event that flowed from her choice, of her decision to be a slave. After all, she usually stayed chained to his home, it did not change much. She was a slave, fully. This was what she wanted. She could not choose to have only certain aspects of this condition. It would be too easy, and no doubt she would tire of it quickly. What she wanted in essence was the constraint, obedience, testing, demonstrating self-denial, against all odds. And that was exactly what she faced. She fell asleep, more or less appeased. She had accepted this situation and decided to devote this time to meditate on this choice of life that was hers.

The next two days were exactly the same. The martinet, applied to the same areas, repeatedly left red and purplish marks on the buttocks. It was mentally difficult to know that it was going to happen, that she was going to be confronted at a fixed time, without possible escape. Duty to afford, without even waiting for an order, just seeing the man arrive. Turn around, and present her ass, suffer, hold back her tears and her cries. And then wait for a few hours before that started again. Apollonia realized that this could go on for days, if not weeks. She had given him this right over her, and he used his right. It was scary at the same time and at the same time ... she liked it. She loved his belonging and that total power he had over her. The fourth day, Monday, she was completely resigned. She had stopped crying. He would come back for her sooner or later. She was his slave. He absolutely had all the rights to her. This certainty had replaced doubts.

†

Her Master arrived in the afternoon, accompanied by the woman with the white veil who was holding the cell keys. She opened the door and Apollonia knelt before him with a pounding heart before throwing herself at his feet. She was happy to see him again; he let her go, looking at her for a long time kissing his feet with self-denial and emotion. She had not stopped at both traditional kisses resting on each of his shoes, she continued uninterrupted, going from one foot to the other, licking the leather, almost out of breath. Greedy of him. He observed also the red marks on her buttocks with a smile. She was so beautiful, completely naked, the body marked, prostrate even to the floor. The soul deeply submissive.

He walked away, and snapped his fingers.

"That's enough. Come."

Apollonia stood up, a little disappointed and worried about this icy tone. He grabbed her by her leash and dragged her behind him. They went back on the stone staircase and crossed large, empty rooms. The white-haired woman was ahead of them, opening the doors; they went upstairs. Apollonia worried, she felt vulnerable as well, naked at the end of her leash in this huge building. They finally entered a cozy lounge. The walls were in wood paneling and upholstered in dark red. There were black leather sofas everywhere, coffee tables in precious wood, huge windows, and large carpets on the floor. Apollonia smiled a moment by imagining the castle of Roissy in Histoire d'O . She quickly lost her smile, realizing that there were a lot of people in this room. Largely men, but also some women, elegantly dressed. And they submitted, some doing the service and carrying also a white veil. Still others, in various outfits often unequivocal, kneeling here and there, probably in proximity to their respective Masters.

Master Vincent approached the man who had accompanied them the first day. He was talking, standing near a window, with another man. He paused to greet him.

"Did everything go well?"

"Yes, very well, she was perfectly wise and docile. Nothing to complain about."

"Good for her."

The man smiled.

"Are you sure you do not want to stay? We have a wide range of entertainment tonight."

"Another time, no doubt. I will definitely need your services in the future."

"With pleasure. Welcome back."

Master Vincent greeted his guest and walked back across the room, Apollonia always at the end of his leash. When they arrived near the large front door, a woman stood ready to open it and handed over a bag containing the affairs of Apollonia, her kit of toilet, her shoes. The return was just as silent as getting there had been. He waited until they returned and he had ordered coffee before talking to her.

"How did you live these days of captivity, Slave?"

"It was very difficult at the beginning, Master, and then I understood that I had to respect your will."

"It is very good. I'm proud of you."

"Thank you, Teacher."

He knew how difficult this prison had been. He had expected her to give up and claim her freedom there, or immediately return. He was looking at her, buttocks bruised and colored red, purple, and black, drawn features. She was so fragile and yet so strong. He admired her dedication. He sent her to shower and get ready to resume her place worthily with a gentle tone.

†

He had to work, that's why the return had been a little precipitate, but he allowed her to stay close to him, curled up to his feet, as she loved being so. He let her wrap herself around his foot. She felt good there, safe and protected. At her square. He felt her quickly let go, and watched her. She stopped talking and fell asleep, so fast. No doubt her nights there had been grueling despite her inaction during the days. She seemed soothed, relaxed. Happy. He understood at that moment that he would not have the strength to part with her in the days that would follow, contrary to what he had planned. There was a lot of constraints, a lot of organization and concerns, but ... it was also a lot of other things in return. It was not just about having a body to take as soon as he wanted sex; Diane was always very available to satisfy him, and then if it was not Diane, he never had the worry of finding a partner when he wanted to. He always had the numbers of two or three subjects without a collar, ready to make themselves totally available to him. It was something else, that extreme submission, that acceptance without limits. This strong will to endure everything for him. It was exhilarating. He liked that. A little too much to be reasonable.

He wanted to reward her for her attitude during her captivity, and spent a long time with her during the evening, allowing her to eat near him, at his feet. He made her catch her food directly with the mouth, like a bitch in her bowl, and caressed her at the same time. She had to stay focused. She felt his fingers coming and going in her, slipping slowly or faster, and lingering where she could not restrain herself from moaning. She wanted to immerse herself in this moment, to savor it fully, but he forced her to eat at the same time, just to see her troubled to have to handle this meal in this position of an animal, and the pleasure he was doing between her thighs. He liked to see her so, destabilized but doing the right thing that was asked. He accelerated the pace, embellishing his gestures with words. He told her as she was soaked she should be ashamed of herself behaving like a bitch in heat, which she was in his eyes, nothing more.

He told her that he liked to see her eat on the floor, at his feet, and that was her place, existing only to serve him and belong to him, that she was his thing, his toy, and that he made her what he wanted. Apollonia writhed with pleasure under his fingers; for a long time she was moaning, jiggling to feel it better in her. She could not eat anymore, so he slammed her ass a few times, for her to submit and obey. Her buttocks were still sensitive because of the martinet. Pain mixed with pleasure, and the humiliation of her situation and his words made her enjoy the brutality. She crawled in an almost animal cry too, and remained breathless, almost ashamed of having taken so much pleasure, just under his fingers. Without even giving him any. He did not let her get up. He pressed her neck to lead her head to the food and ordered her to finish, and to lick the plate, like a well-trained bitch.

He said that only after she begged him could she be allowed to suck his dick. She knew he was watching her, so she licked even more, cleaning the bowl with great strokes of tongue, without any restraint, the pleasure always disinhibited of the modesty that could have remained with her. She gave herself without limits, the rump indecently offered, the loins arched to the extreme, the perverse language. She knew he loved it, and he did not want to tell her, which increased her desire to satisfy him. Once the plate was totally clean, she straightened with a shyness that cut with her previous position; she lowered her eyes, cheeks still red with pleasure and excitement. She begged him to be able to revel on his cock, a little ashamed but with the raw words he liked her to tell him. She stopped talking, slipped between his knees.

She whispered to him that she would be a good sucker, she could play with her tongue everywhere, his balls, at the end of his penis. He did not make her repeat it because he wanted her, and it was a good moment. He surrendered to her docile mouth; she was well trained and knew how to give him pleasure. He had guided her a lot at first, explaining it almost too much, with the lustful caresses and gestures he loved. She had learned the different rhythms she had to take, how to wrap her tongue around his glans at the same time as he came and went on him with her mouth. She had a hard time getting coordinated and doing well, but she was becoming more and more skillful and very applied. He let it go until he felt he could no longer restrain himself from enjoying it. So he ordered her to stop, he still wanted to take advantage of her, her pussy and her ass. He wanted to use it excessively. Wanted to see she could not take anymore, she had enjoyed too much, screamed too much. That her body and her soul were filled with him as much as possible, and that she had reached the limits of her pleasure.

Only then would he catch her by the hair and spill his cum on her face, radiant with pleasure. He already guessed her smile from feeling the hot liquid flowing down her cheeks and chin. He would not allow her to wash herself, not immediately, so that she could be delightfully soiled for as long as possible. Marked by her Master in the most beautiful way.

Apollonia lay on the bed, not even realizing where she was, not that she might have had to leave immediately. She was still breathless. He had never taken it with so much force and almost stubbornness. She had never taken so many pleasures, until she lost her head. She was on her back and smelled his sperm running down her face. She had a smile like an angel.

She was beautiful. He straightened on one elbow and looked at her for a moment. She crossed her arms, sweet and serene, and realized that it did not hurt to stay so. He slipped his finger on her cheek, to recover his sperm, and made her lick all that had flowed on her cheeks. Apollonia did not really like it, no more than another woman. But she liked his look on her, the sweetness with which he touched her chin, and the shine in his eyes when she sucked his finger stained with cum, as if it were the most precious nectars. They looked at each other for a long time without her lowering her eyes.

The bond became stronger and stronger. They both felt it. She had the wet eyes of inexplicable happiness. A tear of emotion ran down her temple. He smiled at her, put a kiss on her shoulder and pressed himself against her body, as if to finish filling it.

Apollonia had never felt so good. Contrary to what Master Vincent thought, despite the difficulty of the test of the "kennel" she had never considered leaving. For her, it was not a possibility. She refused to think that she could give up, just because she was trying. She had not even thought about it.

A slave has no choice but to stay, and she liked it that way. She had felt impossibility, this non-choice. And she liked that. She did not realize that until afterwards, of course, and then it was easier to admit. She felt fully in her condition in his place, and this wonderful moment that he offered her on her return was almost too handsome. She could not help but think that for moments like this, she would definitely return to the cell, offering her rump to the scathing whip. Dinner had started late, and he had enjoyed her body. The night was well under way. After allowing her to go shower and remove what was left of dried semen on her face, he called her back to the room. She lay down on her cushion, closer to his bed. She wished him a good night with stars in her eyes.

Despite the prospect of the deadline, Apollonia was deeply happy; she wore that dreamy steel necklace, the one that would stay a long time at the feet of her Lord and Master. She remained prostrate at his feet, her eyes brilliant with intense emotion. She was his, beyond everything.

It was the only shadow on the board. This date seemed far away, but it would soon become a countdown. He woke her up and made her lie down against him; she did not dare to say a word, not knowing what he expected from her, but he just took her in his arms, and went back to sleep. She did not even dare to breathe, she was afraid of disturbing his sleep. She was satisfied, beyond the possible. Gradually, she finally relaxed, and enjoyed as long as possible the heat of his body against hers, before going back to sleep. Almost in spite of herself.

†

Five weeks had passed since she was here. So little time, but during which so many things had happened. Her life had changed dramatically, and yet she felt no lack. This "before" him seemed strangely far away. Almost unreal. She had the impression she had been there for years, not five weeks. When it was nine sharp, he had her come and kneel, facing him. She kept her head down, trembling. He detached her leather collar and stared at her for a moment before speaking.

"We have reached the end of your month to confirmation. Would you like to stay, Slave?"

"Yes, Master, more than anything."

"You amazed me all this time. I thought you would yield. You did not commit any serious fault, and you served me well. You are a good slave. I have no reason to send you back."

Apollonia felt her heart beating fast.

"I'll keep you. For a year. Not one more day. I am committed to you staying here after that. To help you to return to a normal life, or to help you find another owner, if you prefer to remain a slave. In this case I will give you to him in a year."

"I do not want to belong to anyone else ..."

Apollonia was troubled, she never imagined such a thing. Belong to another? Unthinkable. She was his, not just a slave, his slave, to him, to him alone and to nobody else.

"A real slave can be traded, sold or exchanged, you must know that. A slave does not decide what she wants, or doesn't want!"

"Yes, Master."

"By giving me all the rights over you, you also gave me that one."

"I did not think about it, Master ..."

"You should have."

"I realize that, Master."

He remained silent for a moment, letting her take the measure of his words.

"Reassure yourself, I'll keep you for myself. A whole year."

"Yes, Master. Thank you."

He put a stiff metal collar around her neck, closed with a small padlock.

"The one who wrought it told me he could weld it around your neck so that it cannot be removed. At least, not without great difficulties. But as I do not keep you definitely, I just close it with this padlock."

"Yes, Master."

His words troubled her. To be sold? Surrendered? She was not sure that this was a way of speaking. To sell a slave, even a consenting one, seemed really too extreme. Even for Apollonia. How to pass from one Master to another? How to accept such a thing? And at the same time, he was right, a slave is not supposed to be able to decide what her Master intends for her. She who dreamed of non-choice, it was a possibility that despite everything frightened her.

A return to normal life, or be sold to another? He himself seemed undecided. No doubt he would judge this at the end of the year, depending on how it went. He had wanted to tell her that it was a possibility, that he considered it. But at the mere thought of no longer being his, she felt bad. That he did not want her anymore, that he continued his life as before, without worrying more about her, without any feeling—to leave it to someone else, it was an extreme pain. She had the feeling that he had not even for her the attachment a man has for his dog. All this was so paradoxical. She was there, at his feet, this steel necklace around her neck.

A few days ago, he had taken her to bed and she had read in his eyes that there was something, she was sure of it. How could he simply give in without thinking about it, while this link was going to become undeniably stronger in the coming year? She refused to think more about it and wanted to take advantage of this moment. He wanted her, he wanted her close to him every moment of the day and night.

"I will certainly be even harder with you. The more time that passes, the more I feel you belong to me and I have all the rights on you. I will use and abuse. You will feel your slave condition deep within you."

"Yes, Master, that's what I want, to belong fully to you."

"I will not always take the time to talk to you as I have already done. Sometimes just so you do not doubt that you are nothing more than a slave."

"Yes, Master, I understand."

"Habits and repetitions will not make me less demanding; on the contrary, I think that with time, you have to become perfect."

"Yes, Master, I'm going to apply myself to become perfect."

"You better."

Apollonia was still prostrate at his feet. She was troubled by the ambivalence of his feelings. This duality between wanting to be nothing more than a slave, and that desire, counted little for him. She loved when his words were hard, even scornful, but she also needed these little moments when she detected something in his eyes and in his smile. Master Vincent told her that he had given up the idea of finding her a name, and that he would continue to call her "Slave" according to her condition. That this was finally the name he had chosen for her. The one that suited her best.

PART FOUR

He made her get up and tied her in the middle of the room, to the ring which was fixed to the ceiling and to which he had made several references on his blog. Apollonia had always looked at them with desire, wondering if one day he would deem her worthy to bind her there. The rope wrapped around her wrists forced her to stretch completely, arms in the air. He tied to her ankles a spreader bar, and she found herself perfectly unable to move.

He put on her ball gag and a blindfold and gave her some whips before letting her wait. She heard ringing and recognized Diane who was slamming her stiletto heels on the parquet. She guessed she kneeled in front of Master Vincent to greet him. They ignored her for a while. Apollonia understood from their conversation that they had spent the previous weekend together. It was to be with her that he had made her stay in the kennel. She would have preferred it to be something else, but had finally resigned herself to the fact. And then the conversation took another turn.

"So that's it, Master? Her confirmation period is completed?"

"Yes, this is it. That's why she's waiting like that."

"Can I, Master?"

"Of course."

Apollonia tensed a little, worried. And then she felt Diane's hands on her body. They caressed her breasts, her hips, they wandered all over her skin. She penetrated her softly with a feminine delicacy and stroked her clit at the same time. Apollonia could not believe what was happening. She had always been curious about relationships between women, but without ever trying to taste it. It was one of those things that she said she wanted to do one day maybe, to see, by curiosity, but without really believing it. When she offered herself to Master Vincent she had guessed that she would be faced with that, and she had not seen a constraint on the contrary.

But she would not have imagined it would be Diane, and that it would happen so. Yet he had told her from the start that Diane loved the fact that he lent her his other submissive. Her fingers were getting more accurate, more inquisitive. She was sweet, but without any modesty or hesitation. She knew the body of women well and was soon to make Apollonia moan, who was trying as best as she could to remain impassive. She was offered, unable to move, to see, or to speak. Just a quartered body. A toy of flesh that one lends and that one manipulates. And Diane was playing with her, with fairy fingers. When Master Vincent began in turn to caress her breasts, to pinch her nipples, at the same time Diane was speaking, Apollonia quickly felt that she was going to lose herself, flooded with pleasure. Once again, she yielded to his first desire to remain like marble. She fidgeted quickly under their hands despite her bonds. For once, she was no longer non-existent in their games, but on the contrary, completely the center of attention. She was passive, and they both cared—they treated her body with ardor; it was disturbing. Deliciously disturbing.

She guessed Diane kneeling in front of her and felt her tongue on her wet pussy. She had jerky breathing, was panting. She had trouble swallowing her saliva and regulating her breathing with her gag. She had sore shoulders and thighs, but she liked that contrast, that mix of pleasure and constraint, the sweetness of Diane's tongue, and the pain of her nipples too strongly pinched by her Master. She felt completely offered, helpless, forced to undergo everything without knowing what to expect, and she liked that. She loved it.

Diane drove her fingers in her at the same time as she was licking, she sucked her clit with great skill, and Apollonia did not control anything anymore. She enjoyed a scream choked by her gag, almost unable to believe that she could have taken that much pleasure so well. But Diane did not stop, she seized a vibrator and penetrated Apollonia, while Master Vincent gently whipped her ass. Apollonia was out of breath, she was writhing in all directions, pain and pleasure. And then she felt the vibrator run on her clit and could not hold in a few cries. The sensations were intense, and beyond that, she felt a little humiliated to be so offered as an object. She imagined Diane watching her twisting in pleasure with a smile, while keeping the sex toy where it was needed with formidable precision.

Little by little, Apollonia found herself slowly abandoned and she guessed that Diane was sucking her Master. She remained ignored, as she heard their breath and their groans of pleasure. They left her for so long, without worry about the pain that was getting intense for her at the wrists and shoulders. They were both in their world, the Master taking advantage of his submissive and abandoning his slave.

Finally, Master Vincent asked Diane to detach her, but just the hands. She had to keep her headband and the bar between her ankles. Master Vincent grabbed her by the hair to go on all fours. With the bar, it was complicated and she was forced to move in a funny way, only progressing awkwardly. When he stopped, he took off her headband and put pressure on her neck with his foot for her to bow. She discovered that she was between Diane's legs stretched out. She understood what was waiting for her but being gagged she did not know how to go about it. Master Vincent slapped her.

"You give her pleasure, little bitch!" he ordered her. She felt humiliated but applied her gag on Diane's pussy, daring to press on her clit. She was doing small movements while maintaining some pressure. Apollonia knew well that she caused little sensations as well, but she felt that Diane was giving herself gently.

"Can I release her tongue, Master?"

Master Vincent nodded and Diane quickly detached the ball gag that fell on the floor, full of saliva.

"Work better now!" ordered Diane. With the liberated mouth, Apollonia tried to give her pleasure as best as she could. She had never done that before, but it seemed natural, and rather pleasant. And especially she did not want to disappoint her Master by putting too little enthusiasm into it. She tried to do well, discovering with her tongue the intimacy of Diane, her taste, her tremors in contact with her mouth.

She slid her tongue inside her before coming back to linger on her clitoris. She was hoping to do well so she felt relieved when she finally heard her moan. Diane ended up cuming in her mouth, with a great moan; she then offered herself to her Master who finished giving her pleasure. Apollonia stayed where she was, lips smeared with cum, not daring to do a gesture, until Master Vincent came to free her from the spreader bar. He ordered her to go shower and eat quickly. She finished just in time to return to the entrance and be chained there almost all the rest of the day.

She meditated a long time on her new slave status, confirmed for a year. She was thinking about Diane who seemed that day to enjoy her sexually. She wondered if she would finally have to completely submit to her. Until now, Diane had never given her an order or demanded anything of her. She had always looked a little high and mighty, with sometimes a bit of arrogance, but she had never belittled her, other than by a few looks or amused smiles.

Things seemed different now. She was becoming somehow their slave. Master Vincent had indeed given Diane the right to submit, play with her sexually and demand what he wanted. He had also given her the right to hit her with the whip if she thought she had been badly served. Diane was using this power, but without abusing it, even if sometimes it was a beneficial situation to belittle her a little in front of him. Apollonia did not blame her at all, she knew that her Master liked to see her that way and she ended up thinking that it was in the order of things of this world. And then Diane was not often there, only on weekends, and not always. It was always a test, mentally, but generally, once she was gone, Master Vincent always told her of his pride in her attitude and self-sacrifice. And just for these words, and the little attentions he had for her after, it was well worth it. Through training, humiliation, and hardship, her mind had become stronger. She accepted without any problem treatments or situations that would have seemed unbearable to many others.

†

One day Apollonia saw her Master come in with a big cage. There was still the cardboard packaging that partially covered it and which showed two large dogs of different breeds. And the mention of "Model for large dogs."

Apollonia did not show any particular reaction, but internally she was troubled. The chain was not enough? She never thought that he wished to put her in a cage, alone at home. He had explained many times that he did not want to leave her any freedom, less opportunity to live a "normal" moment. And even less, he would not want to return one day without finding her in his place. She was free to leave at any moment, but she should ask for this freedom. Apollonia had never considered leaving so on the run. She had been surprised that he could consider it. She had been a little destabilized to think that that was partly why he did not want to leave her free to come and go in the apartment. He did not really have confidence in her, nor consciousness of the real gift he had given her. She saw him installing the cage in the second bedroom and then come back to her. He put a leash on her, and made her go on four legs to the cage.

"Enter."

"Yes, Master."

Apollonia had to curl up to fit into the cage. She looked up at him, half imploring, half resigned.

"Do not look at me like that, little bitch. I will be very punctual."

"Yes, Master."

"I will soon be receiving people who are not of this universe. You will do a very thorough cleaning, you will prepare a meal, and set up a pretty table. And then you will spend the evening here, so feel your condition. It will be painful and very uncomfortable, I do not doubt it. But I want to spend this evening vanilla, with classic remarks but by imagining yourself so, just on the other side of the wall. Small bitch in her cage. Just because I want to. You will have interest in being well behaved."

"Yes, Master, I'll be."

"I have no doubt about it. I will leave you here a little, so that you learn your space."

Apollonia did not add anything and watched him leave. She realized how much she had become more and more easily submissive. In a sense she almost regretted her own docility. She liked having to overcome a difficulty, feel a little internal struggle, not have that disturbing moment when she yielded and submitted. Of course, nothing she experienced was innocuous, and Master Vincent knew how to renew himself and surprise her by his perversity. But sometimes she regretted accepting situations so easily when before she was terribly excited by their difficulties.

However, when she had to spend the evening in this cage, while he was entertaining his guests, it seemed less obvious to her. It was rejection and loneliness that overwhelmed her the most. Being locked in a dog cage, in one of the most uncomfortable positions, was no longer really a test, but to be there relegated as a cumbersome animal that is shamed before his friends was particularly trying. But that was her condition, her choice. The reason for her presence here.

He released her once everyone left, and accompanied her to the bathroom. He watched her relieve herself, leaning against the door jamb. Contrary to the logic of thinking, she was happy with this attention. Certainly, to stay before her to see her urinate was meant to humiliate her, but he was there, near her. He gave her his time. He then made her clear the dining table, clean and tidy up while he was relaxing in a bath she had made him according to his orders. When she joined him, he stared at her for a long time, eyeing her, raising his chin. Then he took her by the hair, dragged her with him into the hot water and laid her on his body. Never before had he done that and she savored every second. She felt deliciously good. Such a reward meant that she had been a good slave to him. His carnal contact, the heat of the water, the sweetness of the foam, of his arms around her, his breath on her forehead put her in all her states. It was exactly that kind of moment that deserved all the difficulties, all the solitudes, and answered her doubts. Master Vincent perfectly balanced the attentions he offered her. More would have been too much, less would not have been enough. She smiled, cheek against his chest, intensely happy. This night, after having used her body for a long time, he allowed her to sleep in his bed. In his arms. Her ultimate reward.

†

The next day he made her get into his car again, blindfolded. Like the first time she had to keep the coat wide open, revealing her nakedness. That was how he wanted it, slave exposed. There were many opportunities for her to be seen, but obviously that was what he was looking for. He especially wanted her to have no reserve to offer herself, just because she was his object that he exhibited as he pleased. He finally stopped and ordered her out and to hold her coat closed, but without doing up the buttons. She stayed at the side of the car with her arms tight against her chest, happy— there was no wind. He did not take off her blindfold and took her by the waist to walk near him. She had understood that they were not in the same place as previous, and was relieved, even if standing in the full street, blindfolded, and the coat ready to unveil her naked body at any moment was particularly disturbing.

This proximity and its contact was terribly exciting for Apollonia. She felt deeply privileged to be so close to him in an animated place which she perceived to be. It was strange and indescribable. She could hear without seeing the people they met, all the more so because they did not walk fast. She wondered what they thought of her as they saw her blindfold. She knew that her steel collar was noticeable and she felt very proud of her condition. This contrasted with all those days she spent almost alone and locked up when it was very destabilizing. They finally arrived. A door was opening. It was hot, she heard several people.

Their arrival was planned. A man welcomed them. They entered a room where she guessed that there was already a presence, and Master Vincent ordered her to remove her coat. She took it off as if she was not naked underneath. She had guessed that unlike the last time, the place was not suited to that. She imagined amused smiles from the other men present and yet she remained motionless, her head high, but her heart beating. She felt she was starting to lose her assurance when she heard metal noises she did not recognize.

The man said everything was ready, then Master Vincent guided her to approach a sort of narrow bed and he ordered her to lie down. It was not really a bed because it was higher and much firmer than a normal bed. Apollonia thought about an examination table of a medical office and this did nothing to decrease her worry. She was breathing quickly and her throat was dry, but she was silent because she knew that Master Vincent would not have forgiven her if she questioned him.

Her Master ordered her to spread her legs and then to put her hands behind her knees and keep her feet full in the air, thighs wide apart. She was therefore elongated, totally offered, in that position. She was determined not to disappoint him, but she was clenching her teeth and the uncertainty about what was waiting for her became very oppressive. She wondered if he was just taking her to a gynecologist. The wait did not end; she heard metal noises and running water, but no words, nothing that told her what was happening. When finally she felt hands on her she realized was not at a doctor's, not a conventional doctor, in any case. He fondling her intimate lips, barely penetrated the end of a finger, made her lengthen her legs before telling her to resume her position, and then she felt he was applying a cold product and she realized brutally that she had to be there for a piercing.

How could she have not understood earlier? Barely did she realize that she felt a clip on her lip and a very intense pain, but very brief. It was after, when she felt that he was moving what had pierced her, that she was in pain. With her hands behind her knees she was trying to stay as motionless as possible and clenched her teeth, tears in her eyes.

She was just starting to breathe when she understood that it was not finished, her second lip was entitled to the same fate; she was going to have two piercings, one in front of the other at the level of the entrance to her vagina. The piercer asked Master Vincent if he liked it and he answered that it was perfect. He moved what had hurt her too, but not so much.

The other man, whom she had guessed was in the room, offered a coffee and he agreed, while ordering Apollonia not to move. She stayed elongated, her thighs indecently open while they had coffee. The man gave him some indications for her toilet, care, and time needed to heal. He told him to wait at least ten days before resuming sexual activities. Master Vincent made her get up and they left the living room. Apollonia blew softly; she was not really ashamed to be so exposed, it did not matter to her, she wanted him to be proud of her, nothing else.

The pain was gone and she did not really feel the presence of a foreign body in her. They left as they had come, but this time without the blindfold; without a doubt she would have more of a contrast between her situation and the numerous passers-by of the district of Les Halles. She was relieved not to really hurt, or feel embarrassment. She was careful sitting in the car and had to take a suitable position which was even more indecent with the cloak open. It did not really escape the pedestrians who passed in front of the hood of his Audi.

He brought her directly back to the apartment and she was a little disappointed not to benefit more from this outing. Apart from the time to settle some material and practical details related to her sabbatical one year, she never went out. She did not experience these formalities as an exit, but as a constraint. In fact, she did not like to return to her own apartment, or to her workplace.

She had gotten rid of this as a painful chore. And he had not really left her alone, he had waited for her in the car, thus putting her, voluntarily or not, under pressure to do it as soon as possible. She did not like this return to her former reality, which had made her see her future in a year. Return to this life as before, or remain a slave, leave to be delivered to another? This thought obsessed her as much as overwhelmed her.

Her eyes were always veiled when she thought about it after that, and Master Vincent understood it. He had been considerate with her after this day of external formalities. She had been exactly as he needed her to be. He hit her with the whip so she had no doubts of her condition and quickly resumed her place, her role of slave. And then he had long kept her against him. Tenderly.

†

Once back home, Apollonia was allowed to see her piercings. She had disinfected before him as he watched too. He told her that later he would put a small padlock on to bind the rings and that her pussy would no longer be accessible, as a symbol. He also told her that during the next ten days, he would not penetrate her, so as not to hinder her healing. But because he wanted to frustrate her, he decided that he would not use her in any other way during those ten days. Neither her mouth, nor her ass.

Apollonia resigned herself, head down. She was a little worried about having sex with these rings in case they were still painful during penetration, but he did not deprive her of tasting his cock by other ways. Though she was not fond of sodomy, she loved to feel full of him, and offered him her orifice so that he could use it whenever he felt like it.

She liked that he belittled her by words when he came and went so deep in her ass. She already felt that frustration would quickly become a nightmare, almost a punishment while she had been perfectly obedient. Just to know that she was going to be deprived of sex, she already felt envious. He reaffirmed his decision, and he announced that the only physical contact she would have with him during these ten days would be with his balls, for the awakening of the morning. She could lick and suck them, playing with her tongue, lapping them selflessly until he told her to go make him a coffee. She already felt her belly twist with need to the idea of this certainty that he would not touch her that day, nor the next day, nor the next day. Time passed thus. Apollonia did not get used to being unused sexually, she focused herself more than ever to her chores in the morning while waving her hips and moaning excitement; he simply ignored it and remained firm on his decision. On the sixth day, Apollonia could not take it anymore. Master Vincent had forbidden her to caress herself. He imposed on her to keep her hands tied behind her back to make sure that she would not be tempted, when alone or at night. It was a real torture.

†

"A couple of friends are coming to dinner tonight. We will be four. There are dishes prepared by the caterer in the fridge. You will set up a pretty table and make sure everything is perfect and ready on time. You will serve us. They arrive at eight o'clock."

"Yes, Master."

Apollonia hurried to the kitchen and prepared everything. She set a table elegantly with beautiful dishes and lit a few candles before the guests arrived. Her Master came to join her and ordered her to cool off in the bathroom. Once out, he put on a pair of breast tweezers, less formidable than the Japanese, which he sometimes imposed on her, but she knew they would end up being painful. He tied a chain between them that he passed in the ring of her necklace.

"I want an impeccable service tonight. You will not return to the kitchen between the dishes. I want you to stay there while we eat. Standing in front of the fireplace, hands behind your back. You wait and watch. And if someone needs something, you serve it without hesitation. If a glass of wine is empty, you fill it. I want you to serve us impeccably, that you be a slave whom I can be proud of in front of my friends. Understood?"

"Yes, Master."

"I want you to feel like a fully domestic slave this evening, a simple servant. You will not serve sexually, or almost not."

156

"Yes, Master."

She bowed her head in submission. Nothing was worse than his disinterest and the times when he chose to ignore her. She did not care about the humiliations as long as he cared for her, but the frustration had a bitter taste. Even if she was happy that he did not lend her to his friends.

Diane was there, always sublime in an ultra-sexy evening wear, with a neckline in the back that went down so low one saw the beginning of the furrow of her buttocks. The other couple was very elegant too. The man had a lot of charm, but a hard look. He was in a dark suit and his charisma was no doubt about his status. As for the woman who accompanied him was less charming. She was his subject obviously, but she watched him and he sometimes had gestures and words that betrayed another relationship. Apollonia guessed that they had to have a life of a classic couple, mingled with a relationship of domination and permission at parties or special occasions.

She was not constantly submissive, there was too much familiarity between them. In spite of everything, Apollonia also saw a lot of complicity. Standing in her place, waiting for her services to be needed, she had time to think about what she was watching. She imagined a relationship like theirs with Master Vincent. She found positive sides, but in her heart, she knew it was not what she was looking for. She did not want in any case to feel weakened by some feelings. It was still a complex thought ... but ultimately not that much. She wanted him to love her as a master loves his slave. And not like a man loves a woman. From this Master's love, she wanted to be needed. Sometimes he seemed to read it in her eyes, but so little times. Too few.

The evening was long, she felt useless and a simple spectator. She was not used sexually and if the games of humiliation she had suffered had amused her Master and her guests at first, quickly she had taken the measure of its uselessness during this dinner. The fact that no one could really touch her, penetrate her, or use from her mouth had quickly condemned her to feel excluded. She had supported the pliers, ropes, whip, and belt to entertain them, she had been humiliated and belittled by their words, she had crawled to their feet before licking them, but had not served.

She had been exhibited and exposed as an object without much value that they manipulated a little, before waving her to the end of the room to enjoy the real entertainment, the ones they could take and use, those whose holes they could penetrate, in which they could push their fingers, those that could be slammed in the ass before cumming, those who could play with their language again and again and that never seem to get tired.

They remembered her presence late at night when their bodies had stopped playing, filled for some, bruised for others. When fatigue was great and nobody did not want to get up to get a new bottle of champagne. That's when they remembered the presence of the little slave who was useless, or almost. Master Vincent ordered her with a snap of his fingers out of her corner, so that she got to fill a few glasses, her head down and her position humble.

This evening was mentally tiring, much more than physically. She felt a great void, and her uselessness was transformed over the night into a deep distress. She was leaving to stand her place, having served everyone, when her Master held her back; he made her look up and read her. He always knew how she felt when he looked and she found it reassuring, and sometimes a bit disturbing.

"Stay at my feet, Slave. This is your place."

"Yes, Master."

He had spoken with a sweetness that seemed almost offbeat in context. Apollonia could not hold back a tear that flowed discreetly along her cheek. He alone could see her and she knew that he understood the meaning. Again, in a few words, he had been able to give it this momentum, the answer to her questions.

He had swept away doubts and transformed his sentence into intense happiness. He was at the same time so hard with her, and yet the little he gave it seemed of indescribable value. She was nestling at his feet, where she felt better and she had the chance to collect herself again, to come back to life, like a battery that recharges.

She did not listen to conversations, she was not thinking about anything anymore, she was just fine. Of course, sexual frustration was ubiquitous, but she tried to channel it, to control herself. In a few days, he would take her again, and it would be great, no doubt. Master Vincent leaned several times to fondle her hair gently, as he would have caressed the head of a bitch, and she felt intensely honored by this gesture. She rubbed her face gently against his ankle to express her pleasure to be there.

The guests were leaving and she was carrying their belongings, tired and in a hurry to sleep a little. Diane shared the master bed with Master Vincent, but he also allowed her to sleep in his room, which was rare when she was there. She fell asleep almost immediately, her hands still tied behind her back. She had become accustomed to this and was always surprised to realize how much the body was able to adapt to the constraint, as long as the mind accepted this state.

†

At the end of the ten days, Apollonia could not take it anymore. She felt at once the desire and also the excitement to know that this period of frustration was coming to an end. Master Vincent had fun with her, slapping her even more than usual, doing the chores, voluntarily walking her rump right in front of him, when she was vacuuming, or bending over to clean the coffee table.

He could see that she already seemed very wet, so much did she want him. He knew that physically she needed him, to feel him inside her. He was her hard drug dose, her obsession, and after ten days of abstinence, the lack was terrible. He loved all that power, to control her body, to play with her desires. He controlled her pleasure, her enjoyment. He let it be so, and wanted it more. He made her kneel at his feet.

"From now on, Slave, I'll take control of your pleasure. I want you to learn to control your orgasms. They belong to me as you belong to me. Squirting is a privilege that I will grant you according to my desires."

Apollonia sighed, imperceptibly. She had already heard talk about this stop-and-go technique, often practiced in this world, which consisted of enjoying on order. And only on order. This implied that she had to restrain herself as long as he did, she was not allowed to enjoy, and to manage to let go immediately when he would give the order. She had never really wanted to discover that, but it was a further constraint, a state of fact that would submit her a little more. She was mostly scared not to achieve it, and that the pleasure would be less intense. But after ten days without, she was readier than ever. The moment had been perfectly chosen by Master Vincent who once more testified of this great practice.

Apollonia was nevertheless obliged to note that learning

this technique had good sides. It required a lot of practice. He made her lie down on the coffee table, offering position, and caressed her for a long time, forcing her to control. The first attempt was unsuccessful. After ten days abstinence, she came to orgasm in a few moments, barely had his fingers started playing with her clit.

To his touch, her flesh swollen with too many repressed desires that had sent her brain waves of pleasure; she had arched, and spasms of enjoyment had completely invaded her in an orgasm fast and powerful. She received ten strokes of the whip, heavily worn, inside the thighs. And he started again. He watched her body, each of her reactions, her breaths. He was attentive to her whole being. For to control her body, he had to know it by heart. Know exactly when she was reaching the limit, and when she was able to resist again. The goal was not to push her to the fault, but to teach her to constrain her body and to obey only his voice.

He decided first to force her to restrain herself. Slowing down his movements as soon as she was losing ground and begging him. Under his fingers, Apollonia discovered this aspect, when the pleasure was delicious torture. The sensations were extreme, pure. Live. When she had reached the limit of her abilities several times, and he had to lower the pressure again to plunge it into this forced pleasure, he pushed her further, waiting for her to beg; she shouted to him that she could not, that she was not going to be able to hold back, that it was too good, too intense.

So he intensified again his gesture, pressing barely harder on her clitoris swollen with desire and excitement and ordered her to enjoy, in a dry and sharp tone. Unlike what Apollonia had thought, it was no less good, quite the opposite. She let go completely, in a deep scream, and contracted several times, under the influence of a new pleasure of an intensity unbelievable. She was panting, sweaty, her heart pounding speedily. She had lost her grounds, she was elsewhere in the space of a few seconds. Unable to believe she had ignored it too long as his body was able to provide her with such sensations.

"It's good. You understood the principle. You reacted well. It will always be so now. I want to control everything about you, including your orgasms. Sometimes I will use you without allowing you to enjoy, you will only serve my pleasure. Because I want it. By that a slave does not have a right to pleasure, she only has access to it when her Master offers her this little privilege. Remember this well, Slave, you'll be here for many more months. You will never be my companion, my lover, nor even my submissive. You are my slave, and I have all the rights over you. You are not yours anymore. Because of these rings that mark your belonging, you have been frustrated ten days. I can decide to do it in a month, or two, just so you are immersed in your extreme servitude and of this condition that you came here to seek. If you want to fuck and enjoy whenever you like, leave this place. You are nothing but a slave and I own you, use you, frustrate, or reward you with only my decision. It's your role, after all."

"Yes, Master."

Apollonia stood up, out of breath, troubled by this experience and his words. To contain oneself thus seemed to have increased tenfold sensations, she almost felt her belly contract with pleasure. More than ever her sermon had acted, she felt she belonged to him, his soul, his body, his pleasure. Master Vincent watched her and read in her eyes that she understood what he was expecting from her. She was subject to his goodwill, ready to sexually frustrate for him, if that was his decision. She was his slave. So he ordered her to come and kneel between his legs. Apollonia obeyed with eagerness which made him smile, and looked after him for a long time. Ten days that she had not sucked him. An eternity. She savored every second, treating it with the tip of the tongue, rolling it up, lapping, then sucking it gently, just the glans, turning everything around by aspiring it with a technique more and more elaborate. And then finally, she chocked on it, as far as she could, to the back of her throat.

She had learned to control herself, after many difficulties, and now knew how to welcome his cock deeply in her mouth. Even if she had never again managed to really make a "deep throat" as in the movies, she offered him the maximum from her mouth. She was going up and down slowly, clutching her lips and aspiring while playing with her tongue. Then she accelerated the pace. He put his hands on each side of her head to guide her, to accompany her movements until the sensations became exactly what he wanted. He then took advantage of the heat of her mouth, before seizing her by the hair, turning her around and putting her breasts on the coffee table. She offered herself immediately, knowing that in these cases she had to lay her hands on her buttocks and spread them as far as possible, arched back and open thighs. She had learned all the gestures, and he appreciated her perfect position, her abnegation total.

Gradually, her body became an object of pleasure without fault. She was not just a woman who let herself be owned as a sex slave, trained to his pleasure. Every part of her body was calculated and measured, every gesture was dedicated to the pleasure of her Lord and Master. She had adapted to all his desires, to all his preferences. He had nothing left to say, just a gesture, a look, a beginning of movement, and she knew what he wanted, what to do, what position to take, what attention to lavish on him.

He spread her lips delicately to accustom himself to her

piercings; she was always soaked and he slipped easily into her. He quickly realized that past the apprehension at first, she did not suffer at all, and he accelerated his movements, sinking into her with delight after this period of abstinence. He had often wanted her, but he was not one of those who yield to the impulses, thereby losing their own decisions. Although the need was sometimes very strong, especially when she purposely tried to tease him, he did not look like he ever had the temptation to yield. He considered that to control others, it was first necessary to know how to control oneself perfectly. He was a Master of himself, before anything else. But the ten days of healing had passed, and he had wanted to use his slave. Very much.

He enjoyed her for a long time, taking her by all her orifices, preventing her from enjoying according to his new rules. He liked to see her twist with need, to hear her begging, almost on the verge of tears. He liked to look at her, when he allowed her to give in to pleasure in a liberating cry which left her destabilized, and a little lost for a few seconds. He liked to see her, her cheeks red, her eyes sparkling, panting. He liked to hear her thank him, just a troubled whisper before moving her ass again, liked her to beg; again, he did not deprive himself to give it to her with great thrusts.

He did not yield to his own pleasure when she could last no longer, she was only a body without strength or energy, so often he pour his cum on her face or her belly, and was feeding on that spark that shone in her eyes. Pure happiness, to be able to serve him and give him some pleasure. A gift of oneself, sincere and precious. She was in her place in those moments, intensely. She felt it most deeply in herself. He kept her against him, for a tender moment, so she felt that she counted for him. She was satisfied.

Her slave life was, however, a land of contrasts.

Sometimes he woke her up in the middle of the night by pulling her by the hair; he penetrated her mouth almost violently while she had not even opened her eyes yet, and took her thus. He possessed without letting her move, hands on either side of her head, guiding her movements. He used himself in pleasure, wanked with her mouth. Without a word, without a return.

He was squirting his sperm deep in her throat, after an eternity of back and forth ankylosing her jaw. Then he pushed her back brutally in a heavy silence before leaving, and leaving her almost dizzy. She was an object to his service. Nothing more. A body at his disposal. An orifice where he could freely pour his cum. Why should he have constrained himself to a few words or a little delicacy, if he did not want to? She was there to serve him, only, without compensation or return. And it was well so. She went back to bed, often with a smile. Happy to have given him pleasure, no matter how.

†

It had taken more time than Master Vincent had thought to really get used to her presence and to treat it without it ever being a constraint for him. Owning someone like that was less simple than it seemed. Like a pet, you always had to look after it a little, think about it, make sure she had enough and had enough to drink while he was not there. She had to find something to renew the days, and it was in that, mainly, that he thought she did not act like a real slave. To ensure her well-being, a minimum of three quarters of an hour daily sport to compensate for long periods of inactivity were practical concerns, even essential, if sometimes painful. But this concern to offer her moments and different sensations betrayed his desire for her not to weary, something that ultimately he should not have to give. If he did not want to spend time imposing props on her, or slamming her buttocks with a paddle when she did the housework, he did not have to do it and that's all. If she got tired, well, she could leave.

The period of the first times was past, it was initiated, well trained. Everything was in place in her body and in her head. She knew what to do and always fervently applied to obey and to do everything he wanted from her with passion. But she was obviously occupied less. She had got the realization but remained helpless against it. She could not give him more than he did not ask, or self-discipline to bring him even more he did not want to. She was passive because of her slave status.

Master Vincent was also aware of the situation. He hesitated between letting it go, taking the measure of its commitment and drawing the consequences, or choosing to spend more time to take care of her, even to go beyond the status of a slave. After everything, he did what he wanted with her, even if it was for him to give more attention than necessary. He decided after a few weeks of being a little distant, to benefit more from her and from the gift she had given him, for the few months that she would remain his. He watched her preparing a dinner. She was just starting and he interrupted her.

"Stash all that, Slave. I want to eat outside this evening."

"Yes, Master." She bowed her head and complied.

"Go dress, I'll take you."

Apollonia looked up at him, her eyes so sparkling that she was tearing. He did not regret his decision. She had to of course keep her collar on and wear an indecent outfit, but it did not matter to her; on the contrary, she was proud to go out so with him, like his little private whore.

They walked for a moment, getting lost in the streets from the Odéon district to the covered walkway at Saint-André-des-Arts. He took her to a small crowded restaurant, typically Parisian. Apollonia was more than happy to be there. Not only because she finally came out after months of confinement, but to be with him, that he wanted to after those weeks. They ate together, like a couple, except that she always addressed him with deep respect, punctuating each sentence of the word Master. He was amused to see her sparkle with happiness. She was an excellent slave, she deserved that, as he had wanted her to. Why force himself to leave her, if it was what he really wanted? They both enjoyed this dinner with the aura of the first time, and it was rare that they spoke together so long, so "normally," even if she did not find interest in his words.

He pushed her to reveal herself, to tell him more. She had no secrets from him, she belonged to him and indulged him without a mask. She answered all his questions, without shame nor detour. She spoke to him of her life before as a bad memory. From this constant sensation to be nowhere than in his hands. From this lack of permanence which she did not know how to put into words up until to what she discovered in this world.

She told him the revelation that it was, her deep addiction to his new fantasies. She answered all his questions so precisely, he who so perfectly blemished the emptiness she had always felt. He told about himself a little too, very little, but more than never. He outlined the highlights of his life. A divorce, the choice to remain free to live, the submissive which was revealing of his desires for domination. That evolution which dragged him further and further, to the point of wanting a slave. They exchanged an intense look, which said much more than the words. They had found each other and they both knew it.

This evening was the first, but later, it was more frequently that he allowed her to go out with him. He took her from time to time to do some shopping, having fun getting into trouble in fitting rooms or anywhere else. He sometimes walked her on a leash at night, and from afar she just seemed to be standing by his side; an observer would have seen a chain of steel joining the necklace without forcing that adorned her neck in her Master's hand. She loved it. She loved this new twist in their relationship. And the same if he continued to be sometimes very hard, probably to counterbalance those moments of attention; she was fully happy.

He kept her against him more and more often. Offering her tender, almost cuddly moments she loved. In these moments, she drew the strength she sometimes needed to accept everything else. She was getting better, she was filling up on him from the bond that united them. A delicious complicity was settling as time went on. She felt she counted on him and savored this feeling intensely.

†

One evening in July, after a late night out in a chic bar on Saint-Germain-des-Prés, they made their walk last, strolling in the streets. Intensely proud to walk by his side in Paris by night she loved so much. She wanted him, a desire that had nothing to do with reason, which trembled her belly and obsessed her. A desired animal, excessive, unspeakable. A need to be taken, to be fulfilled in the true sense of the word. A desire to feel him in her, to feel his cock penetrate its full length in her body. Wanting to shout with pleasure under his hips, feel his hands grip her, feel him take her without delicacy, to excess. Excessive.

But she was not sure he was still doing her the honor of taking her because he had used her body in the afternoon.

She savored this walk at night, his presence beside her, his words, his arm around her. He paused for a moment to pull the leash out of his pocket. She could not hold back a smile, while stretching her neck toward him so that he attached this leather leash to her collar, a reflection of the invisible link that united them to one another. They continued their way; nothing seemed different, but it was. She felt deep inside herself. She had lowered her head, her breath had accelerated. Her sexual desire gave way to her pleasure to feel submissive. She did not feel humiliated to be thus kept on a leash; far from it, it was for her a real pride to be so; treated by him.

They left the busy streets where she was having fun trying to detect in the eyes of passers-by what they thought in seeing her. Her Master dragged her away from where she thought they were going, toward a small Parisian park which was without doubt deserted at this hour. Her excitement grew suddenly; she had already guessed a special moment when her submission would be put to the test. She felt capable of a lot, full of what she had already given him. More than anything she wanted his approval. They exchanged a smile as they saw a sign at the entrance of Park: No dogs, even on a leash.

The place was indeed deserted. Master Vincent brought her in, and she followed him obediently, wondering what he was going to ask, with fear, but also with the hope that he pushed her toward a difficulty that she could overcome. He raised her dress to discover her buttocks, and quickly she had to go on all fours. The grass was wet but she liked it. She felt like a dog. His dog. He made her walk a long time as well, and as soon as he stopped, she also marked the stop, as she should, her cheek stuck to his leg. She inspired fun, enjoying her condition as it was rarely the case. The moment seemed suspended, almost magical. She was good, in her place. And then the order fell. She was a dog, and like a bitch, she had to relieve herself.

He ordered her to urinate, right now, on all fours like a little dog well trained. She was not really surprised because she had read these practices on different blogs, but she felt a shiver go through her whole body. She contained herself not to show a reaction or hesitation. She remained a little frozen, concentrating on obeying and remembering the road traveled, and how much her mind was fully in the acceptance of such an order. At no moment did it occur to her that she was not going to obey, or that she could not accept such a test. She was his. She was his bitch. However, her body did not yet have the faculty to react as it should spontaneously. Fortunately, her Master let her handle this ambience between acceptance of the mind and resistance of the body. He remained silent, waiting for the execution of his order, so she could concentrate.

The seconds passed and seemed to last an eternity. She was beginning to feel bad about not doing it, fearing his disappointment. She was planning to ask him to allow her to squat instead of remaining on all fours, aware that this unusual position was largely responsible for her difficulties. Yet, her desire for obedience took over and she managed to constrain her body. She began to urinate, the curved neck just ahead of her Master's feet, thighs open. She imagined her white butt slicing in the darkness of the night, just illuminated by this lamppost which diffused a trembling light. She knew that buildings surrounded them, and that Paris did not ever really sleep, windows were open, but she was not really worried who could see her. She was with her Lord and Master, nothing else mattered. A noise not far from them still made her jump slightly but she was not afraid, he was there. She obeyed.

She could not tell if she felt ashamed. Would she have been ashamed to obey and satisfy her Master? She was beyond the act. She was in pure obedience. Obedience without question, without apprehension. She no longer belonged, she was no longer herself, just a body with orders, a soul submitted. And she liked that, she liked to feel this abandonment, these extremes, these acts probably a little "borderline," but who tied them so strongly. Meet his expectations, whatever they were, to know themselves without limits for a few moments and to feel something new. Feel that he knew exactly what she was going through and what was going on in her mind, while she herself was not really aware of it. Get to surrender to him, entirely, blindly, and with confidence.

She was not ashamed, no. She was rather proud to manage to obey, but it was not insignificant, far from it. A first time that marked as a freeze frame on her evolution and its learning. Little bitch, on all fours in front of her Master, her ass in the air, which relieves itself in the grass wet, without being ashamed. Impossible to understand for those who would stop at the gestures. But at this moment, the incomprehension of others was the last of her concerns. She knew what it was, and he too. The rest didn't matter. Their link seemed to her only stronger, more anchored in something deep. She felt boundless.

She had finally finished. Not being ashamed did not make things easier so far; she had the feeling that the moment had lasted an eternity, which ended up making her uncomfortable and impatient to continue this walk tonight. She finally rubbed her cheek against his leg and without a word, he pulled on her leash and dragged her a little further. She moved forward, always on all fours. She was in a different state, in his bubble, conscious of her condition. Deeply conscious and grateful for the honor he bestowed on her by allowing her to discover and push her limits thus, at his feet. He made her straighten up and approached her. She did not dare to look up to him, but she guessed he was satisfied with her. His satisfaction was her reason for being. How to take pleasure. Pleasure pervert without doubt, but a form of pleasure anyway.

They went back and she walked by his side, as when they came, but she was not quite the same anymore. She needed for a moment to accept what had happened, to integrate it and become fully aware of it. She had the feeling that the embarrassment she felt was going to stay more or less omnipresent, but after a few minutes her Master was able to put her back perfectly at ease. After everything, she had only obeyed him. Once back, she went to shower and came back kneeling at his feet, little bitch obedient and grateful. He knew how to reward her beyond her hopes for her unwavering self-sacrifice. Each of their outings was punctuated by a difficulty or an exhibition, however small it may be. It was never a simple walk of a vanilla couple. He remained her Master and she was his slave. He always made sure that she did not doubt that it was otherwise. And she was fully happy.

†

For several weeks, Apollonia had noticed the absence of Diane. She was not coming on weekends anymore, and Master Vincent was staying more often at home, or going out with Apollonia, which delighted her to the highest degree. She had tried several times to question her Master, but she felt deep inside that it was a misplaced question. A slave does not question her Master. If he had wanted to talk to her about it, he would have done it. She knew that he did not keep his submissives for several years. There had been some before Diane, there would be others after her. She was in no hurry to discover the next one, and took advantage of it to be alone with him. She knew her status apart. She redoubled her efforts to satisfy him and give him pleasure, she wanted more than anything to suffice him. She was perverted every time that she had the opportunity, giving him everything, and more. She offered herself with such greed and self-abnegation that she was beautiful and touching in her devotion. She deserved her place, undeniably.

When he finally judged her worthy to accompany him to the club he loved to attend, she was no longer the same. She was metamorphosed by these few months of slavery, obedience, and constraints. She had acquired a posture naturally arched and walked on her high heels with ease, without even paying attention. She had done this by practicing, and especially by noting that her Master always wanted it so much, and even more and more. He loved her body, he liked that she gave him pleasure. It meant that she was not insignificant, nor faded. She was worthy of him. This simple observation gave her a brand-new assurance that was visible in her eyes.

She was proud of her condition, proud to belong to this Master who held the tip of her leash. And that night, it was she that everyone followed when she wandered around the club, too, finally on conquered land. She remembered her look at Diane, the first time she had seen her, how beautiful and full she had found her of grace. Today she was there. She may not have a body as perfect, such a pretty face, but it was not what really counted here.

She had the look, the gestures, the support which imposed. She was there, slave, in her place, in this world she had dreamed of so much, and she knew that she would make the pride of her Master by her exemplary obedience. She knew he did not doubt for a moment that he could compel everything that would pass through his head. She knelt beside him, elegantly, without rushing, without clumsiness, gestures with the ease finally acquired many executed times.

Master Vincent found some friends and spent a long moment with them. He allowed Apollonia to take a cup of champagne, and she remained so, docile, savoring every second, and measuring the path traveled with a smile on the lips. She was wearing a little black leather dress, very tight. A zipper on the front allowed to open it fully, and Master Vincent had lowered the slide to her belly button so that her cleavage was most plunging. One could see her nipples point, sometimes, by the crack that was created according to her movements.

She wore stockings and very high boots. She had also mittens in black lace. She had enjoyed herself a lot when she looked in the mirror before coming. She had become aware of her new seduction, she was surer of herself. She was found beautiful, and had thought probably horny, in the eyes of a man. She never really dared to judge herself thus before, at least so explicitly. The look of her Master finally convinced her. She had read their admiration, for her, his slave. She was now ready. As much physically as mentally.

One of the friends of Master Vincent, a man not really beautiful, without being ugly, but without charm, looked at her with excitement for a moment. He was quick to compliment her Master on his choice in subject matters. He replied that she was his slave, and without really explaining himself, Apollonia felt very proud of this distinction. Not that she could derive that one was more rewarding than the other, but because she was the only one to have this status. She felt apart, privileged. Different. He quickly ordered her to entertain him and his friends with a lascivious dance. Another young submissive who accompanied a domina was invited to join her, and both of them launched into a duo more and more torrid, not hesitating to caress each other and kiss each other. What should be a simple distraction that enlivened the conversations was very quickly the center of attention, and well beyond the table they occupied.

Apollonia sometimes dared look at her Master, and saw him smile. She guessed him proud of what she had become.

The evening continued, Apollonia was tied on the cross of St. Andrew. Master Vincent had taken off her dress, she was wearing her garter belt, her stockings, her heels, and her mittens. She had no modesty, no fear. She indulged, body and soul. He pressed himself against her back, and told her he was going to hurt her. Very bad. Because he wanted to, and not to punish her. She was there for his pleasure, so she had to submit and make one proud by one's abnegation. Apollonia was concentrating; she had never been very masochistic, even if she would have liked to be, this being associated with the image she had of a slave of ancient times, regularly whipped, beaten.

She had tried to convince herself that she liked the pain, but it was totally utopian. Being hit made her feel wrong. Just very badly. Nothing more. No physical pleasure. When it came to small strokes, it was not unpleasant.

On the contrary. She loved that he whipped her back gently with the swift when he took her, but it was not about real pain. Real pain was when the shots were really worn, when the leather bite was so stinging it seemed to lacerate the skin, so for a moment, nothing counted, just that feeling of being skinned alive, and this pain that remained, spread, long, radiating.

Furthermore, the tears rising, the body trying to deal, despite the pressure of the spirit. All that disappeared; for a second, it was too loud, too difficult, too much pain. All this came back to her in a moment. She was preparing to face that. Because she knew that after, he would be proud of her. Just for that. She knew that once the pain passed, she would feel stronger to have supported it. That she would be a little disappointed, too, to see that despite the pain, her body would not be marked as much as she imagined. Far, very far from a laceration. Even if it sometimes happened that the shock of the leather on the skin raised a little blood, but it was rare. Master Vincent very rarely hit her so hard. But it had already arrived, never to punish her, just for her pleasure, just because she belonged to him, and that he did what he wanted with her. He put a few kisses on her shoulder and Apollonia felt stronger. It was as if to remind her why she was offering herself so.

He hit her with a short whip, on the buttocks, the side of the thighs, and shoulders. Apollonia was tense, she knew she was not supposed to be, but it was too difficult. She could repeat the words that were making a loop in her head in those moments ... It's useless to be afraid, it's useless to cry, you just have to give up, give up ... she had a lot of it, but it was hard to stay as impassive as she wanted.

She thought always that she would arrive there, in her memory, the pain always dissipated a little; she even wondered how she could have hurt so bad, but at once, she remembered. Everything came back. There was only pain, violent, like a shrill cry that hit her skin with force. It was the first time she was treated like this in public, and strangely, it gave him more strength. She did not want to be weak in front of others, she did not want to cry, scream, or squirm, let alone beg him. She wanted to stay dignified, support her head high and admire everyone, so that he was prouder of her than he had ever been. Four shots ...

It's useless to be afraid, it is useless to cry, ten blows ... just surrender, surrender ... thirteen strokes, it serves nothing to cry, just surrender ... nineteen blows ... to abandon oneself, to abandon oneself, to abandon oneself ... twenty-five blows ... surrender ...

More a noise, more a movement, she waited, suspended,

hands clenched on the leather bracelets that held her prisoner. She was contracted like never before, all that he did not have to, she knew, but how to avoid it? And finally, his hands on her skin. The touch of his chest, along her back. His lips against her neck, his voice to her ear ... "I am so proud of you ..."

Probably because this world was full of contradictions, it was not the whip that made her cry that night, she had held back her tears all the way. It had been his words, so delicious to hear, that made her cry. Just a few tears of emotion mixed with an intense smile, which shone like diamonds on her cheeks. He took her off and she dropped to his feet, keeping her face glued to his knee. He ran his hand through her hair and stayed for a long time like that, letting her enjoy those moments, and without a doubt also for him. He dragged her with him and sat on a large red velvet armchair, where he was when he accepted her request. She slipped between his legs, and put her head against his thigh. He kept her against him, it was time to witness the spectacle of another body on the cross.

Apollonia did not really look, she was elsewhere; right after that was following a moment of great difficulty but she had been able to face it with her head up. She had made him proud and she would have damned herself for that. It was a little bit that she was doing by offering him her soul. He kept her against him, letting her savor her condition. He gave her a few tender gestures, then a little later, he ordered her to suck; she complied without embarrassment or restraint, reveling in this as a reward. He did not honor her so much of her pleasure, but compelled her to make her mouth enjoy two of his friends. It was the first time he had lent her that way. She showed no reluctance, but found the ordeal almost as formidable as the whip. It was difficult, even more than giving pleasure to Diane. She would have liked to be only with him. She would have wanted him to not want to see her with another. But she discovered that he had no problem with that. She obeyed. Without desire, but she was putting a lot of effort into it for him, not to reproach him for anything, but he knew. He had read it in her eyes. And probably just for that, he forced her to apply at length. He was not testing her ability to give pleasure to another, but her obedience. Her pure obedience, and without flaws. Whatever the order.

When he felt that she had sufficiently demonstrated her abnegation, he signaled her to return to him. She kept her head down. She felt submissive; he was satisfied with her, and it was essential. She just wanted to move on. She realized that she would never be able to belong to anyone other than him. She understood how it made no sense. She offered herself to him alone. She could not and would not give herself again. Out of the question. The idea that Master Vincent could consider selling her troubled her. She would have preferred that he make her swear on her life that she never belong to another. She would have found it normal and right.

The more time passed, the more the ultimatum was approaching, and the more she was anxious. She did not disappoint him during the evening. He was aware of her dedication and his slave's qualities. All those present that evening had seen her and many had told him so, but they had remained discreet about wanting her. It was up to her Master to congratulate her and reward her if he wanted to. They did not talk to a slave.

Once they got home, he dragged her into the shower with him and ordered her to wash him. It was rare that he did it, generally preferring her to wait, kneeling. It was the favor he gave her and she felt it deeply. She soaped his whole body, slowly, rediscovering the gestures of the slaves of yesteryear, slaves from Egypt and Rome, from the East or from Asia, dispensing their talents for their Lord in ancient baths. These images mingled with her reality, she was in his world. Her imagination had conjoined her real life. She was the eternal slave. She touched him with veneration, as a sacred idol, like the demi-god he was in her eyes. She rubbed herself gently to him, stroking his skin with her own body, with her breasts, her belly, and her thighs. They undulated, in a rustling of the bodies, in a sort of trance, like a lascivious dance. An erotic ritual.

He did not tell her anything, nothing was explained. It would not have been useful. She had naturally behaved thus, as if it had always been anchored in her. It was obvious to her. Her role as a slave to her Lord and Master. She slid her hands all over his body, while continuing her carnal caresses with her breasts, folding her knees to go up and down against his hip. In support on her thighs, she positioned herself so as to feel his cock just between her breasts. She lowered her head slowly and gently licked the tip of his glans while continuing to rub, to brush it. She had never felt so sensual. She was almost troubled by this closeness, this freedom that he let her go through his body. It was not the first time, but that night, after the intensity at the club, after the whip, the pain, the strength of her feeling of submission, it was like the pinnacle of something. A deeply rich and intimate moment that further strengthened the bond that united them. She felt in the depths of herself and in her Master's gaze. She read emotion too. She was reading something that words could not translate.

When she thought it was time, she adjusted the water to the ideal temperature, and rinsed his skin, without hurry, always with great delicacy. And when that was done, without him saying anything, she knelt down and licked his body to dry it, starting with his feet, delighting with each of the caresses she gave him, lavished with her tongue. She was taking all her time, so slowly along his legs, lapping every drop of water. She lingered even more on his balls until he turned around, so she slid her tongue between his buttocks. Not knowing finally if it was him or her who took the most pleasure in this rose leaf. She ended up back again, between his shoulders, she licked his neck, standing on tiptoe, almost timidly, as it looked like kisses that did not really belong in their relationship. However, he sometimes offered them, to encourage her, to reward her, and even sometimes without reason. She hesitated, she felt like it, just for a moment she stopped licking his skin and put her lips on it, delicately, preciously. He let her go, but she was not sure that this was correct, given her condition.

She then resumed her spirits and having no more water to lapse on his body, she went out and took up her kneeling position, tending the bath towel, in case he still had the use. This was not the case. He put his finger in the ring of her necklace to make her get up and looked at her for a long time before leading her onto his bed.

He made her lie on her stomach and caressed her back, buttocks, and hips, where there were marks already almost violet of the lashes he had brought her a few hours earlier. He did not speak, it was not necessary. Some silences say more than words. Both felt the intensity of the moment. He played with all her holes and used them, without violence, just for his pleasure, to finish this night with her moans and her muffled cries. To own again her body. She gave herself as much as she could, drawing on her last strength; he was deliciously disturbed by her enjoyment. She came against his body like a fearful little animal. She did not repel him; on the contrary, he welcomed her against him. She snuggled up against her Master, satisfied. The silence was not heavy. Yet, without her realizing, the words escaped her.

"I love you, Master …"

She had not planned anything, it came out of nowhere; she bit her lip and stopped breathing, unable to know how he was going to react.

He said nothing, but moved a little more against her and put a kiss on her forehead. She calmed down, and finally felt happy to have told him. It was so obvious. She fell asleep almost immediately.

†

Despite this particularly intense evening and the confession of her feelings, nothing different happened during the days following. Master Vincent was neither more nor less hard than most of the time. He did not tell her whether her words were displaced; on the contrary, she had the right to express to him what she felt. Apollonia did not know how to interpret that. She wondered if in her heart she had waited or hoped for something. She told him that she loved him in a very impulsive way, without any premeditation. So she concluded that no, she had not hoped for anything. But afterwards, she realized that this night had been different. She had suffered the whip, she had accepted other cocks than his in her mouth, she had been perfectly docile and a good slave, she had told him that she loved him. And ... nothing changed. Nothing would ever change. She understood that he would never give her more than he already gave her, whatever she did. And that was also her role as a slave: accept it. Of course their complicity became stronger and their link more powerful. She felt that, she knew he was offering her sometimes delicious moments of tenderness that nothing had forced him to give her.

But time was running out, bringing it inexorably closer to the end. And that made her crazy. She could not understand that he could not want her, so easily, just because the time had passed, when he had brought a lot of things together. She felt helpless. Whatever the way she demonstrated her abnegation, the outcome would be the same. He would release her at the end of this year of slavery. Without feeling—neither suffering nor not suffering. She found it unfair, even though she had always known this rule and she had accepted it. Without a doubt, part of her hoped that during the year, she would have made herself sufficiently indispensable and endearing for him to decide to keep her longer. Unconsciously, she did not lie, she had hoped to be different from others, to be the one he would decide to keep, against all odds. Against his own rules.

She was watching him sometimes, and understood that he would stick to his decision. She resented him. And then she looked at him again: he was so handsome, so charismatic, so many things. She was looking at him and realizing she was close to him, that she was lucky enough to be a part of his life. She knew that despite everything, he would never forget this little slave who had shared his life for a year.

She knew they would stay in touch after that, maybe, he would agree to see her again from time to time. It was already a lot. So she blamed herself for those negative thoughts. She was unworthy of what he was giving her in wanting more.

She went through all stages of reflection. Happiness, deep and sincere, to have been able to live this experience she had dreamed of so much, to the deepest despair to think that soon, everything would be finished. She felt more fragile, more emotional. When he was tough with her, she thought, what was the point, since it was soon over, and when he was tender, she found it almost unfair, because it made her already almost nostalgic, in anticipation of what she would never live again. Her behavior was affected by all these reflections and moods. She did not seem so devoted and motivated anymore. She did what he ordered, but something died a little in her. She did not realize it. At first, she had given herself without counting, with fervor and passion overflowing, to please him, to make him want her. But the closer the end of their story got, the more it seemed to her in vain. Whatever she did, he did not want her anymore.

Master Vincent was not fooled by all this. He knew she was affected by this deadline. But he did not like this change in attitude. One morning he brought her near him. She was watching him sadly, as if to pity him, and he thought it troubling of her condition.

"Do you know what day we are?"

"Tuesday?"

"Yes. We are almost on the 8th."

Apollonia looked down.

"In a month, you will have come to the end of this year of slavery."

Silence. Apollonia knew that if she had spoken, she would have melted in tears. She wanted to be strong, but it was beyond her strengths.

"You are a good slave. Really. That does not give me pleasure to give you back your freedom. I have gotten used to your presence, even if sometimes it was complicated to manage. You will leave a big empty aura here at home, when you're gone."

He let her immerse herself in his words. The silence was heavy.

"Until now, you did everything I imposed on you with a lot of strength and with dignity. You accepted everything, endured everything. The pain, the loneliness, the bonds, the humiliations. You had exemplary behavior as Diane. You have endured much more than I had imagined, and I believe that few women could have done it. For that, I'm very proud of you, and happy to be your Master. I ended up believing you without limits, and thought you were really capable of everything for me."

"But I am, Master!"

Apollonia could not believe that he doubted her desire to endure everything for him.

"No, you are not capable of everything. You are not without limits. Your abnegation is not total. You are not really a slave."

Apollonia was in shock, unable to believe he could say that after all she had done and accepted for him. She felt a physical pain deep in her chest, and her emotion already present mingling with a kind of anger and feeling of injustice that knotted her throat. Her hands were shaking and she felt her heart beating fast in her chest. These words were like a slap, powerful and terribly stinging. She did not understand.

"Your limit is this end to come."

She looked up, both amazed and at the same time reassured. He was not unfair. He did not minimize everything she had given him so far. He was right.

"A slave gives herself without limits. Dignity, even in pain, whether physically or mentally. A slave accepts everything from her Lord and Master. All. And this applies to giving the best of herself every moment. I gave you one year. What we agreed upon. Do not disappoint me now. Do not ruin everything. Or, leave right away. But if you stay, take advantage of every second. Give me the best. Make me proud to the end, until the last second, respecting my will. The will of your Lord and Master. Be perfect, as you have been until now, every moment. Show me that your abnegation is true and flawless, and that it was not all just a game. A real slave does not have her own desires, except to please her Master. So forget your own desires and satisfy mine. Until the end of our contract. That's what you got involved in."

"I beg your pardon, Master. You are right …"

"I want you to meditate on it, to think about it. That you understand in the depths of you the meaning of my words. You do not just have to agree because my words are consistent to your commitment, I want to see that you really feel that at the bottom of your heart, as a new and last evidence."

"Yes, Master, I understand ..."

Apollonia was too troubled to express herself without letting her emotions show and preferred to remain silent, head down. Her Master dragged her into the little room. He never took her there, except when he wanted to lock her in her cage. She went on all fours. He blinded her eyes and tied her wrists behind her back. She had to curl up, her knees bent under her breasts, with her hands tied behind her back; it was extremely uncomfortable.

"I will let you meditate on my words and your condition."

He left, leaving her alone. For a long time. Apollonia was completely destabilized. She knew he had reason, but it was so difficult to accept. Maybe it was true that she had limits. Only one limit: accept to no longer be his. Nothing was harder than that. She cried on this end to come that she could not accept, on her abnegation that was not flawless, on the disappointment she caused. On her inability to detach herself completely from this suffering that was hers, as soon as she thought of the after.

Could she pretend it did not touch her? Could she really not pretend, but show an altruism totally toward him? To play a scene, which she could have, very certainly, would be lying. To show her spirit, her submission, without looking sad to depart: it was possible and it was probably what she should have done, but what's the point if it were not sincere?

He had imposed on her the absolute truth, to surrender herself naked. Each time, do not play, be yourself ... She stayed a long time in the dark, to comprehend all this, to try to convince herself to succeed. But deep inside her, she knew it would stay feigned. It was not just about being a slave, it was also about the feelings she felt for him. She loved him, sincerely. Master, but also, inevitably, the man he was. When he came back for her, long after having locked her up, she was aching, her makeup had sunk, she had a face of one who cried too much. He tied her to the ring, to the ceiling, and then knocked her hard with his whip and his belt. Alternating the two so she never knew what pain to expect.

The blows were not as painful as the whip during his club outing, but they were more numerous. She was not staging. Her resistance would not impress any spectator. He did not do it out of desire, but to make her react and punish her. And that was the hardest thing to endure, being punished for her thoughts. He watched her body curl and twist. She could not escape his blows, but she could manage to refrain from trying.

He was looking at her back, buttocks already red. He passed in front of her, and looked at her breasts, before hitting them too. He saw her chest lift up at full speed, her belly, her hips, he watched her pussy, always perfectly smooth. Always at his disposition. Her neck, so fine. And her face, her mouth, to the lips always colorful that she was biting to try to restrain herself from crying again. He looked at her red hair falling back in front of the black band that covered her eyes.

He found her beautiful. More beautiful than ever. So fragile. So loving. He wanted to tell her how easy it was for him to separate from her. He would have liked to tell her that he, too, loved her in a way, as much as a Master can love his slave. He knew that she would have given anything for these words. But without doubt she would not understand. No doubt she would then have hoped even stronger that he keeps her. He did not want to go back on his decision. He was a Master, not a man.

He took her off and dragged her on all fours into the room, holding her by the hair so that she followed him. He threw her on the floor and slapped her several times. He constrained her mouth, holding her by the neck so that she could not back off enough to resume easily her breathing. She sucked him furiously, eager to give as much as possible, to show him that she was still able to give him pleasure, to make him cum.

He made her return to the bed, head back to take her throat. Never before had she managed to offer herself enough so that he penetrated her completely, but this time she knew how to do it, she surrendered like never before, and felt her body open up to him also, as if something in her had really let go. He made a few comings and goings and felt, beyond her mouth, the last of his cock penetrate her throat. He stopped after a few thrusts, and she had to straighten up suddenly to catch her breath, troubled by this strange sensation. He turned her over brutally to take her, he wanted her, to possess her, without half measures, without limits.

He unceremoniously gaped her buttocks, and penetrated her ass in turn, fucking to possess again and again in the depths of herself. She gave body and soul for his pleasure. He did not grant her the right to enjoy despite her supplications. He slammed her buttocks with force and she remembered how many times she had fantasized that alone. She wondered if she would not have been better to live with nothing, than to have known that, and not to ever taste it again. And then he slipped his fingers into her mouth; she loved it, she licked, sucked. Delighted until she lost her mind.

She had no regrets. She was happy to be his, and would be forever happy to have been with him. Never again would be the same. She would stay with him, even if he did not want her to. She was his slave in the soul. Nothing would take her away from it. She loved him. She would have liked to enjoy this love, this belonging and condition, more than just the pleasure it gave him taking her as he did, with power and animality.

She lost her ground, as often when he dragged her beyond pleasure, forcing her to control her body until it became a torture. So he really had the sensation to possess her, completely, her body, her soul, her spirit. Her heart too. He knew it. At that moment, he felt the right to life and death on her. He waited for her cries and begs to reach their climax, and at last liberated her by an order: Orgasm!

And she immediately let herself go in a violent orgasm,

jerky, immense. She was out of breath, her body exhausted. He grabbed her by the hair so that she took back his cock in her mouth; she knew he was going to cum and soon regained her strength. She applied until she felt his sperm fill her mouth. While still sucking it gently, she knew that soon all this would be just memories, that she would never again taste him in her mouth, so she realized that he was right, you had to enjoy every second. Without lament. She did not have the right to find him unfair, he had never hidden the truth. She had accepted it. He wanted to make her understand that despite the end that approached, she should not relax her efforts and remain as devoted as she had been until then. Stay, Slave, until the last second.

She understood his words and his attitude. She tried not to disappoint him anymore. Things were different, undeniably, but she was stronger although she did not look like it. She knew how to cope. She found this momentum which had progressively failed her and showed itself under her best day. He knew how to be grateful for her efforts, and spent a lot of time with her. Often to play with her body and have fun, but also simply to enjoy her presence. And the month passed thus.

†

Master Vincent was sitting in his room, leaning against his bedhead. He called her and made her sit between his legs, her back against his torso. He surrounded her with his arms. They could not see each other and it was probably better that way. She was hugging his body, as if she wanted to be one with him, no longer able to be dissociated from him. She was immersed in every second which bound her again to her Master. Every second that passed dragged her to what she dreaded so much.

She had made so much effort during the previous month

to live up to his expectations. Perfect until the last month, she had been without question. He had nothing to reproach her for, on the contrary. She was a good slave. Even though he knew she was not totally self-sacrificing because she still did not accept this end in its depths, she had to mask her pain and give her body and soul to the end.

"It's tomorrow."

"Yes, Master. I know." Her voice was already whispering.

"How would you like it to happen, if you had a choice? I mean, sincerely, not what I want to hear, the true desire of a woman."

Apollonia let a few seconds pass, she had not felt like a woman for so long. He had never used that word to talk about her. She would have wanted him never to consider her as anything other than his slave.

"What would I really like? That you change your mind, Master ... you tell me no, you do not want me to leave. Then you would remove the padlock from my necklace of steel, and we would go together to the one who wrought it, to let him tie it to my neck. And I will stay with you."

Apollonia realized she could not even cry anymore, she was empty inside, beyond suffering. The words were out painfully from her mouth. He squeezed her a little more in his arms. Silence settled in, but it was not heavy. All was silent around them. The room was in a semi-darkness, the day was already ending.

"May I ask you, how is it going to happen, Master, really?"

"I'm still thinking, between simply freeing you, or you quit yourself. Do you have a preference?"

"I wish it ended as you want. I will respect your will until the last moment. That's what you asked me. This is my reason for being."

"So I'm going to organize your sale. I want it that way."

Apollonia finally felt a tear run down her cheek.

She had a heart full of sadness. Master Vincent was talking softly, in a calm voice. It was almost a whisper in her ear.

"I would like one last evening worthy of this year, in our world. I do not want to take you home by car, carry your suitcase to your studio and greet you in the footsteps of your door. I do not want to see you leave my house either like that, and imagining you're disoriented in the subway. I want something else that puts a worthy end to this history. A transition. Tomorrow we will go to a club, I will call some of my friends to make sure there will be potential buyers. I will have to honor myself. I will announce the sale and conditions.

All this will of course be symbolic, but will really mark the end of your belonging here. It will be a very tiring time for you. But you will feel deep, demented Slave, perhaps more than you've ever felt, and maybe for the last time in your life. Buyers will come observe you closely, they will feel you, they will search your holes, they will make comments without worrying about what you think. They may ask me to test your mouth, or slide their cocks in you a few moments, for you to taste, test yourself. I will undoubtedly accede to their requests.

You will feel lowered as ever. Then I will sit down, and I will publicly make a demonstration of your abilities and your obedience. You will obey all my orders, knowing that they will be the last you receive from me. Then you will give everything, you cannot disappoint, but on the contrary, to make me proud of you, as much as it is possible to be for this last time. I will hit you and will degrade you before all those people you do not know and among which will be a buyer, your future owner. Can I let the manager of the club manage the auctions, I know that he does that very well? You will probably be completely naked, standing, legs apart and hands on the head, you will be worthy and magnificent. I want you that way. I will join the buyers and I will watch you throughout the sale. I do not want any tears, no mark of weakness. I will be very proud of you. Auctions will rise gradually, and the final price of your sale will be reached. So I'll congratulate your new owner. He will necessarily be known to me, and someone I trust.

You have nothing to fear from that. I'll give him the key to your padlock. You will not be his, unless you want him and him too, of course. But you'll be his for the rest of the night. He will do what he wants with you, in the club. I will still be there, not very far, but you will not be mine anymore. I know you'll do what will not disappoint me. When I leave, you will not cry. You will kneel and you will find the words to thank me for this year. You will be strong. This Master who will buy you will take you home early in the morning, it will be agreed so. Our roads will separate with dignity, without weeping, without crying, as you came to me, in our world. In this club where we knew each other. This is how I would like our story to end."

"So that's how it will end, Master ..."

Her voice had broken. There was nothing more to say. It was useless to fight, to beg, or even to pray, all was organized, planned, relentlessly fair and true. Apollonia was in a second state, she did not really realize what was going on, it was too difficult. So he straightened up a little, and prompted her to turn to him. He made her raise her head with his finger under her chin, and kissed her. For the first time. For the last time. A kiss, much longer than she could have dreamed. She discovered the contact of his lips against hers, the heat of his tongue that penetrated her mouth; she would have given anything to make time stop. He had slipped his hand behind her neck and with the other, he touched her cheek. It was like a kiss of a fairy tale. Apollonia did not dare to breathe anymore, she got wet—she was born for him, with all her being. It was way too short. He pulled back slowly and got up to go shower.

He allowed her to wash him. It was the last night they spent together, just the two of them, and she would give him every second. He took her to the restaurant. They did not talk about the next day. They did not talk about the after. They both were as if nothing was going to happen. She sometimes found in his look the things he did not say. She refused to understand that. Nothing forced him to release her, it was his choice, his decision; she would not have been able to tell him how difficult it was for her. No doubt he knew it.

They walked long in the streets of Paris, as if he wanted to remind her all she was going to find tomorrow at the same time as her freedom. But Apollonia did not have the heart to do that. She did not guess anything good about the coming days. The return to her previous life was not going to be a succession of painful stages where she would be bitter—the statement of all that it would no longer be. Master Vincent did his best to have a good evening, she felt, and she appreciated it. Nothing obliged him to do that.

He took his time, once the night was well settled, to use

still her body, and make her enjoy his. He ordered a massage; she knelt down first at the foot of the bed where he was lying on his stomach, completely naked. She dared then fully to look at it. She was enjoying the moment to detail and soak up every inch of his body. She started by spilling some massage oil into her hands and she rubbed his feet for a long time, with delicacy but assurance. She knew he loved her actions. She went gently down his legs, passing from one to the other, walking her eyes on his buttocks, his back, his shoulders. She had wanted him. Irresistibly. She felt it between her legs, at the deeper part of her belly. She massaged his thighs, kneeling on the bed, above him. She was coming up slowly, rubbing her tits to his butt while her hands were already busy from the bottom of his back. She ended up astride on his hips, doing her best to relax his shoulders and neck. She liked to feel so at his service, that was her place, she knew it at the deepest part of her soul. She did not understand that he could not see as clearly as she did.

He turned around and made her lie down on her back, keeping her thighs wide open. She offered herself without any restriction. He settled over her mouth, a knee on each side of her head so she could lick his balls. He let her do that for a few moments then ordered her to caress at the same time and to raise her legs. He was enjoying then caressing her tongue, at the same time as his middle finger was slipping and rolling on her clit. He saw her already excited, wet lips of cum. He heard her moans deliciously troubled by the attention she put in to honor correctly with her tongue. She sometimes shook with pleasure, when his fingers were too accurate, almost in spite of herself. Probably because it was their last night she felt his body claiming her even more than until now; she could never have believed that possible. How was it possible so much to desire someone?

She felt her body escape, she lost control, she waved and moved further apart. He had grabbed her ankles, one in each hand, to keep them as far apart as possible, but it was not really necessary, she in no way sought to evade this exhibition. But she loved to feel the touch of his hands on her. She stretched her neck to pass her tongue everywhere, up to his ass. He moved slightly, to allow her a rose leaf. He liked that and she too, she had never had one. She had even been a little surprised the first time he had ordered it. She loved his body, she revered him and reveled in all that he allowed her to see, touch, or taste. Whether it was his ass, his armpits, his toes, she loved everything, she was greedy and eager for him as nobody else. He dropped one of her ankles and slid his fingers into her, into her open pussy, offered whole, boiling and glistening with desire. She was soaked, soft and hot.

He was sticking his fingers in her to put pressure on an inner part of her body that he had made her discover, and which always gave her a senseless pleasure as soon as he ventured there. She knew his instructions, and had not stopped to caress her swollen clit. She found herself overwhelmed with pleasure and excitement; she could not, for a moment, keep playing with her tongue, she was trying to resist orgasm that he had not ordered but it was beyond the possible.

He did not want it at fault that night, especially not, so he acceded to her entreaties and allowed her to free herself from this pleasure that she could no longer contain, and she enjoyed in a scream, all her body contracting completely before falling again, breathless and panting. She just took the time to thank him, and without even taking a breath, she continued to play with her tongue and lips on his balls. He had abandoned her pussy to caress her breasts and play with her nipples, but she had to keep her indecent position, he liked to see her like this, offered, just because he wanted to.

He passed from her nipples to her ass, fingering at length to make sure it would be comfortable, when he wanted to push his cock. He wanted the seduction complete, by all the orifices and all the ways possible.

He ended up ordering her to get on all fours and to suck; she hastened to obey. He lay down, and took advantage of her mouth long before, catching her by the hips and bringing her on him. She did not understand what he wanted but she let herself be guided. She still had his cock in her mouth and he put his knee on the other side of her. She was not breathing anymore. He had never granted her favors of his language.

He told her that he never licked his submitted. Never. But it was different, no doubt, since gently, she felt the warmth of his lips on her pussy, a delicious contact which made her lose her footing immediately. She did not coordinate her own movements any longer, she just wanted to enjoy these magical moments. She felt his tongue slide on her pussy; her clit was already terribly sensitive. She savored every second, every movement, conscious of the honor and the privilege that it granted her. She was definitely not just one of the others, and he wanted to make her understand it by this divine offering.

She was not thinking about what she was doing, sucking him instead mechanically. All her attention was directed to the sensations she felt. He allowed her to indulge in the pleasure in an abandonment more and more wonderful. She wanted to resist the enjoyment, so that it did not stop, for this moment to last eternally. But she could no longer restrain herself from moaning, her pleasure was as much physical as mental, she slipped toward sensations beyond what she could have already lived, and her body finally gave in to the expert language of her Lord and Master.

She enjoyed a stifled moan, fully aware of the value of this gift he had given her. He said nothing to her, and did not reproach her for having enjoyed without waiting for his order. It was a present. A reward for her abnegation. A farewell gift, too. Apollonia refused to see him like this, not to taint her pleasure and this wonderful reminder with the slightest veil of sadness. He made her turn around and grabbed her by the hips, as she loved as much as he did. She was terribly receptive and almost trembling with this abundance of pleasure.

He knew how to channel his own long desire, alternating the penetrations between his mouth and pussy to make it last. He finally sank gently in her ass. He knew she did not like it, but she was his, more than anything else and let herself be taken, eager for all he could give her. Little by little, pleasure came, a different pleasure, but she did not care, she loved everything about him. All he had given was precious and sacred.

He accelerated the pace and she guessed that he was going to enjoy this way; she gave herself more. She told him that she was his slave, that he had all the rights over her, that she loved to feel his cock in her. He retired at the last moment after having allowed one last enjoyment. He poured his cum on her back and buttocks, in a rattle. She remained motionless, savoring the heat of his nectar that was slowly flowing down her curves. She loved listening to his fast breathing and aura of pleasure he had just then. She knew that she had given pleasure. She had the feeling that she only existed for that, for his pleasure.

She did not want to think of anything else this night. The night that was almost over already, so late it was. Both their antics had lasted. She fell asleep snuggled in his arms, without even wondering if that was his will, almost as if it were a due. As a matter of fact.

†

The morning passed like many others. This time nothing had happened at nine, he had not asked her if she wished to renew her vows of belonging. This time, it was finished. He made several calls; Apollonia understood that he contacted his friends to make sure he did not end up in a deserted club and have to leave with her, or leave her to the first arrival. She did not really know what to think of this attention. She would have liked him to be more present, but he went away a few hours in the day. She found it hard, even though she was aware that he had given her a lot the day before. She would have liked to spend every second she had left with him, curled up at his feet.

Evening was approaching. She resented him for letting her love him so much, afterwards to get rid of her so simply, knowing that besides, she would do everything to make it easy for him, without tears. But it was her time, she knew since the beginning it would be so. The next day, she would no longer be his. She would not be the same anymore. A submissive without a collar, a slave without a Master. A body without a soul.

She had the feeling that a part of her was going to die that night, in this club where she had felt born. She should mourn everything she had been and she would not be anymore. Time was passing too fast, and not fast enough. She almost wanted to finish, no longer be in this endless waiting that dragged her to the nothingness. Yet in the evening, after he had taken a long time one last time, she felt like she had not had the time to prepare mentally. The last hours had gone at full speed.

She found herself in front of the club door, almost dazed. She did not even remember the journey, nor did she remember getting dressed, everything was blurred in her mind. The evening went as he had described it. An evening improvised with the complicity of the club manager. Four dominants had come to discuss her price at the invitation of her Master. She recognized one of them, Master K, who had come to dinner at the home of Master Vincent, while she was forced to abstinence because of her piercings. He was not accompanied this time. She did not know the others. She did not care.

Master Vincent spoke with ease and explained very simply what it was, the symbolism of this private sale, the rights and duties of the purchaser. The buyer would have Apollonia for the night, and should drive her home early in the morning, released from his necklace. Apollonia was completely naked except for stockings and a pair of Louboutin that he had offered her a short time before. She had a sad face but remained dignified. She tolerated all the exhibitions imposed on her, leaving the four men to play with her body to test the coveted goods. She obeyed all that was asked of her, took all the positions that suited. She felt like a rag doll.

She thought he looked dark and could not stop wondering if it was her attitude that disappointed. Around her, the atmosphere was more about party and fun. This kind of selling was probably tiring for the slaves, but it was a great entertainment for the masters who took the opportunity to play with docile bodies. Some, by their words or gestures, some showed themselves particularly scornful with her, but she did not care.

More others, who were not buyers, also took advantage of the situation for touch and to have fun with this woman-object offered. There were a lot of people eventually. Masters and submissives, but also dominas, slaves and even passing people, curious, who were not of this world but who had wanted to discover it for an evening; the club was open to everyone. That night, they did not have to be disappointed, the atmosphere was good, and such a slave sale was not trivial.

When Master Vincent thought it had lasted long enough, everyone took a seat on large sofas, clearing the central space where she was offered. He showed her, hitting her buttocks and her breasts with various instruments, to demonstrate her resistance, and then he made her walk long on all fours, and take all her imposed positions, to show how she was well trained and obedient. She had no failures, but did not take pleasure in obeying. She was not hurt much. All this was just an act in her eyes, a game. And she had never wanted to play.

She took her sales position, standing, legs spread, hands on the head. She did not really listen to what was happening, she had difficulty realizing that all this was true, she refused to think of her work, of her life before, she would have time well after. She found it very cruel and perverse, the idea that her Master had had. She did not want to end this evening in satisfying another man, obeying another. Did he do it to disgust her for it to be less hard? Or did he just want to show her that another way not envisaged was possible, with another Master, and that she might still feel the pleasure of submitting to the future?

The auctions went up in small amounts, to make the pleasure last, no doubt. Apollonia knew that generally, when a sale was organized, there were several slaves put on price, and that each could judge their value in comparison with others, depending on the amounts exchanged. S

he thought it had to sometimes be very hurtful. Especially since before the sale, they were often put in competition, to highlight their qualities. It was definitely a difficult test psychologically. No doubt she would have amused herself to compete thus, if it had been a real entertainment for her Master. But his case was very different. She felt a tear flow along her cheek and did not dare to move to wipe it. She struggled to not collapse, so as not to disappoint him at the last moment.

"Two thousand six hundred to the left, and ... two thousand and eight hundred on my right. Two thousand eight hundred once ..."

Apollonia looked in front of her; it was Master K who had the most bidding and who seemed about to buy her. She felt a little reassured, since she knew him a little.

"Two thousand eight hundred, twice!"

She scanned the room, to see him. She did not know what was reflected in the expression of his face. She expected to see pride in his eyes, but it was not the case. She did not know how to interpret what she read in his eyes. She looked away, then she raised her head and stared at him. She would remain dignified and head high to the end. That's what he expected of her, and he was her purpose. He could never say that she had not been a good slave.

"Three thousand."

All turned, in general misunderstanding. Apollonia felt her heart leap in her chest. Master Vincent had raised this auction. This sale was symbolic; nobody, and even less Master K, amused himself to outbid. There was a noise in the background, people were whispering. Apollonia was looking at him, not daring to move, she did not understand. She dared not understand for fear of making a mistake. And then he approached her. He slid his hands on her forearms, and smiled at her.

"It was you who was right. I do not want you to leave."

Apollonia remained speechless for a long time, eyes full of tears of happiness, a smile that was worth gold on her lips. She knelt and wrapped her arms around his thighs, her cheeks against him. She pressed hard against his body before he gently guided her head toward him to remove her steel necklace.

"I belong to you, Master. Mind, body and soul."

Their eyes met and each could read the other in their gaze, the depth of this unique bond that was theirs, as powerful and as indefinable. A link finally much more unwavering just like this steel necklace he caressed gently, and which soon be sealed forever around her slave's neck. For to be free means choosing whose slave he wants to be.

THE END

ABOUT THE AUTHOR

Born in 1988. Ashraf Elia is an architect, writer, and author of the debut novel Limerence. With over a decade studying the principles of design and the history of the fine arts for his degree in Architecture, he obtained a uniquely gracious voice that shines through on the importance of fundamental legacies. His work was published in 15 countries and helped his passionate and curious nature to get lost in new worlds. He has traveled extensively around Western Europe, learning about the history of the region and walking the paths of his characters.

Printed in Poland
by Amazon Fulfillment
Poland Sp. z o.o., Wrocław